Y.A.

YOUNG ADULT

W•CLARK
PUBLISHING

You Got Me Twisted
by
Gloria Dotson-Lewis

Wahida Clark Presents Young Adult
60 Evergreen Place
Suite 904
East Orange, New Jersey 07018
973-678-9982
www.wclarkpublishing.com
www.wcpyoungadult.com

You Got Me Twisted
ISBN 13-digit 978-1936649-45-7
ISBN 10-digit 1936649454
Library of Congress Catalog Number 2012913338
1. Young Adult, Contemporary, Urban Fiction, African American, – Fiction

Cover design by Nuance Art: nuanceart@gmail.com
Interior book design by Nuance Art: nuanceart@gmail.com

Printed in United States
Green & Company Printing and Publishing, LLC
www.greenandcompany.biz

Dedication

This is dedicated to young ladies and men everywhere who have been abused or violated. Don't let the memories steal your joy.

Acknowledgments

I want to thank my heavenly Father who continues to bless me each and every day with the breath of life. You said in your word that if I keep your commandments I'll receive the gift of eternal life so I'll continue to serve you until the end.

I want to thank my husband Marvin, who after all these years still makes me laugh. I love you so much and couldn't image life without you. Thanks to my beautiful children, Deonte, Porshay and Malik, who always bring me so much joy, I couldn't love you more.

Thank you to all my family and friends, each and every one of you hold a special place in my heart. I cannot express how much I love and appreciate you.

Thank you to my NMH co-workers. I couldn't work with a better group of people. Thank you all for your support.

Last but not least, a special thanks to the bookstores, book clubs, websites, and fans that have or will support my books. Thank you, thank you and thank you.

chapter 1

Makenzie parked across the street where she could get a good view of the front door. An hour had passed before Jordan's mother came rushing out in her black, knee length pencil skirt and short sleeve blazer carrying her Louis Vuitton briefcase. Makenzie slid down in her seat and waited until she heard Mrs. Davis' car drive off.

Makenzie had tried calling Jordan every day, but he never answered his phone once. She knew if she just had a chance to talk to him, she could convince him that they could get past their latest drama. Makenzie believed his mother or his boy Devon was in his ear, telling him not to answer her calls, so she decided to pay him a visit.

Jordan's car sat out front. The freshly washed, black Charger was sitting on sparkling five star chrome rims. Makenzie knew he had to be in the house. She pulled the overhead visor down and brushed a fresh coat of Mac lip gloss over her lips. She exited the car, walked up the steps and rang the doorbell. She combed her fingers through her shoulder length streaked bob and waited on him to answer. She made sure to leave the house looking like new money. She had on a taupe and red floral romper she picked up from Forever 21 last week with her matching red peep toe platforms. Her nails and toes were on point and her necklace, earrings and bracelets gave her outfit that extra pop.

"What the hell are you doing here, Makenzie?" Jordan shouted.

"You wouldn't answer my calls. I had to see you. I know people are trying to keep us apart, but we can get past this if you just hear me out."

"Ain't nothing you can say to me to convince me to take you back. We're over," Jordan said.

"Just like that, Jordan? I don't believe you. You can't love a person one day and get over them that easily. You must be worried about what your boys will say if you stay with me. Forget them," Makenzie said as she waved her hand like she was swatting a fly.

"Look, I don't know what you don't understand about it's over but maybe you'll get this." Jordan stepped back and proceeded to close the door. Makenzie pushed it with all her strength catching Jordan off guard, sending him stumbling back. As the door swung back to the wall, Makenzie spotted a girl sitting on the couch looking in her direction.

"Who is that, Jordan? Is she why you've been tripping on me? It's only been four weeks and you got some other chick in your crib already?" Makenzie felt like her heart had just been ripped out her chest and ran over by two eighteen wheelers rolling at high speed.

"Not that it's your business but yeah, you've been replaced. Now, get it through your head and stop calling me and don't come by here no more."

"You know you're nothing but rebound, right? He's just using you to get over me," Makenzie rolled her eyes at the dark skinned girl with long hair who was looking at her like she was green with three eyes.

"Jordan, do you want me to leave?" The girl asked Jordan, ignoring Makenzie.

"Yeah, that's a good idea," Makenzie said as she pointed towards the sidewalk.

"Naw Shayla, she's leaving," Jordan said. "You need to be gone. Step back so I can close my door."

"Are you serious? You're choosing her over me? I look

better than her on my worse day," Makenzie yelled as she stepped over the threshold into the foyer.

"Look, you don't know me so I advise you to get to stepping like he told you." The girl stood up and walked towards the door.

Jordan stood between them trying to keep things under control. Shayla was a little taller than Makenzie. She wore dark fitted jeans, a burnt orange v-neck t-shirt with orange flat slip-ons. She stood with her hands on her hips as she and Makenzie had a staring battle.

"What am I suppose to be? Shaking because you got up? You don't know me either. I'll stomp you in the ground," Makenzie yelled as she pointed over Jordan's shoulder in her face.

Jordan struggled to keep the girls from each other. He gave Makenzie a shove, attempting to get her out the door. She winced in pain as her back hit the edge of the doorway. She was pissed. Her body felt like an oven on five hundred degrees. She quickly stepped out of her shoes, balled her fists and started swinging out of control. She accidently hit Jordan in the jaw as she tried to reach over his shoulder to stick his new chick. She paused for a second to make sure he was okay. Although he was acting stupid right now she felt a little remorse for socking him in the face. Jordan wasn't acting like Jordan and she knew if she could just talk to him alone he'd come back to his senses.

"Why are you still standing here? Didn't he tell you to leave five minutes ago?"

Makenzie couldn't believe this chick was still talking. She wanted to mess her face up but Jordan kept blocking her shots. She felt possessed by an evil spirit that wouldn't let her stop until she got a piece of her. Makenzie finally got a punch past Jordan landing it right in Shayla's eye. He grabbed Makenzie around the waist and lifted her in the air as she continued swinging and kicking at Shayla. Jordan finally got her to the porch and dropped her on her butt.

"Get your crazy butt away from my house before I call the law. You already know you ain't even supposed to be over here anyway," Jordan shouted. "Get up! Get off my property!" He said, as he stood over her with his fists clinched tight.

Makenzie smirked when she noticed Shayla holding a hand over the left side of her face. She slowly stood up as she kept her eyes on Jordan. As many times as they had gotten into it, he had never hit her, even when she was striking him. But, he had a look in his eyes that she had never seen before that made her a little nervous. She slowly backed down the stairs as she held on to the banister.

"Give me my shoes," Makenzie shouted when she reached the bottom of the stairs.

Makenzie ducked as the heels came flying in her direction. "When you realize that bum chick ain't got nothing on me and wanna come crawling back, don't even think about it. I'm too good for you anyway," Makenzie shouted as she got back in her car. She did everything in her power to hold back the tears forming in her eyes, including chewing on her tongue. After starting her engine, she rolled her window down then stuck her middle finger in the air as she pulled onto the road and drove off.

chapter 2

One month earlier . . .

"Makenzie Nicole Pierce you are charged with damaging personal property. This is a very serious offense and I don't take it lightly," the square faced man in the black robe began.

Makenzie's full attention was on the judge who held her life in his hands. She hoped he didn't recognize her from last year. Her sweaty palms were clasped together and her legs quivered as she stood behind the defense table with James Spencer, the lawyer her parents hired to help with her case. As far as Makenzie could tell, Mr. Spencer had done a good job pleading her case but the expression on the judge's face didn't look to be in her favor.

Mr. Spencer gently touched Makenzie's trembling arm to try to soothe her as they waited for the verdict. His hand was warm and soft and his nails were perfectly manicured. His buttermilk skin, green eyes and dark wavy hair, inherited from his African American and Caucasian genes, made him look like he should be ripping the runway on BET instead of practicing law.

Minutes seemed like hours as she waited not so patiently to hear the judge's decision. He flipped through some papers in front of him as she struggled to sound out Kowalczyk on the name plate sitting on his desk.

"You have no previous offenses so I'm going to release you to your mother today," he said as he continued reading from her file.

You Got Me Twisted

Makenzie smiled and took a deep breath.

"No wait, I'm wrong. Here's a sheet I missed. You were in my court room just nine months ago young lady for battery." He looked at Makenzie over his small, black rimmed glasses. "Oh yes, I remember you now. You entered Jordan Davis' place of employment at the Foot Locker, picked up a gym shoe and started beating him in the head with it. The manager had to call the police after you refused to leave. I see you don't take the law very serious Ms. Pierce. Well, today you're going to learn just how serious it is," he said as he began to write.

Makenzie rubbed her sweaty palms on the sides of her pants as her eyes began to water. She couldn't believe that she was about to go to jail for something so petty.

This is all Jordan's fault.

Makenzie Pierce, you are sentenced to one year probation and are hereby ordered to pay $500 to Jordan Davis for the damages to his car. I'm also ordering you to stay away from Mr. Davis. Do you understand?"

"Yes sir." Makenzie took a deep breath, relieved at the outcome. She turned around to glance at her mother who was sitting behind her. Rhonda Pierce closed her eyes and looked up towards the heavens to give thanks.

"I'm not done yet," the judge said sternly.

Makenzie's smile disappeared faster than a cheetah chasing its prey.

"I also hereby order you to see a psychologist once a week for the next six months. It's obvious you have some anger issues that need to be addressed. I've seen girls like you in here before and they usually end up behind bars. So, I'm going to do you a favor and order you to get therapy and maybe, just maybe that'll get you on the right track young lady. And, I will be following up with the therapist to check on your progress."

"I don't need to see no shrink," Makenzie said as wrinkles formed across her forehead.

"Makenzie let me handle this," her lawyer whispered in her ear.

"Would you like for me to lock you up now Ms. Pierce? That can be arranged."

"No, I'm just saying--"

"Then, I advise you to be quiet and listen very carefully because if you end up back in my court room for anything, I'm slamming the bars on you," he paused and stared deeply into her eyes. "You need someone to help you figure out how to rechannel your anger in another way. You can't go around spray painting cars because someone upsets you. If you can't talk it out then you need to walk away," the gray haired judged lectured.

"Yes your honor, I understand," Makenzie quickly answered.

How was I supposed to know the girl riding with him was his cousin?

As the judge signed the court documents for the case, Makenzie tried to make eye contact with Jordan but he wouldn't look her way. She needed to talk to him . . . to apologize and make things right. The judge banged the gavel, snapping Makenzie from her thoughts.

"Well Makenzie you got lucky today. Judge Kowalczyk can be really tough. But, I know you'll stay out of trouble so you won't end up back here, right?"

"For sure," Makenzie said as she looked past Mr. Spencer at Jordan leaving the court room.

Makenzie and her mother headed towards the exit. Jordan and his mother were walking twenty feet ahead of them.

"Mom, can you wait for me in the car? I want to

apologize to Jordan."

"The judge told you to stay away from Jordan."

"I'm just going to apologize. Chill out."

"I'll wait over there but make it quick," Ms. Pierce pointed towards the vending machine sitting against the far wall.

"Yeah, yeah," Makenzie said as she walked away.

Mckenzie picked up her pace to catch up with Jordan. She worked her way through the crowded hallway, nearly knocking down a small elderly lady with a cane. She pushed the double door and stepped outside.

"Jordan, can I speak to you for a moment please," she asked.

"Didn't you hear the judge? You're not supposed to come near him. Besides, he doesn't have anything to discuss with you Makenzie! I can't believe that you would do something like this," Jordan's mother responded with her hands on her hips.

"It's cool mom. I'll give her one minute to speak her peace and then we're out." Jordan walked towards a set of stairs to allow them some privacy while Makenzie followed.

"I've been trying to call you to apologize all week. I'm really sorry for what I did Jordan. But, I don't think I'm the only one at fault here. I thought you were cheating on me. If you just would've called me to let me know that your cousin was over and kicking it with you, none of this would've happened," McKenzie started.

Jordan's sandy complexion turned red as one of his eyebrows raised. "So is this supposed to be your apology? Wow, you really are a lunatic. You spray painted 'busted' all over my car in red because you thought I was cheating and now you're saying it's my fault? Luckily my neighbor saw you and called the police or you probably would've got away with it," he shook his head in amazement.

"It's not that serious. You act like I busted out your windows or something," Mckenzie yelled.

You're crazy! Lose my number and don't ever come by my house again or I'll call the cops," Jordan ordered before storming off.

"I know you're upset so I'll give you time to cool off and think about things because again, you could have texted me and told me what was up so…"

Jordan shook his head then turned and walked away in the midst of their conversation. "The judge was right in ordering you to see a shrink. You act like someone hit you in the head with a bat."

Makenzie smacked her lips. "Whateva Jordan." She couldn't believe how Jordan was blowing this whole thing up.

My mom is going to pay him the money to get a new paint job so what's the big deal.

chapter 3

Makenzie and her mother walked into the back door of their three bedroom home. The kitchen was spotless except for a bowl sitting in the sink that Makenzie had used for cereal that morning. Ms. Pierce was talking to Makenzie but she was too busy blocking her out to hear a word she was saying.

If you don't shut up talking to me I'm going to snap. This is what makes me go off. You talked the whole ride home and you're still talking. Shut the hell up, deg. It's $500, not $5,000. Get over it already.

She darted up the stairs to her room to get away from her mother. She closed her bedroom door and placed her iPod ear plugs in her ears to drown out her mother's lecture. It had been a long day in court and she wanted to go back to sleep.

She positioned her pillow against her headboard and leaned back. Makenzie closed her eyes and bobbed her head to Trey Songz. She didn't hear her mother enter her room or feel her standing over her. When Rhonda Pierce tapped her thigh she started flinging her legs like a fish out of water.

"My gosh Makenzie it's just me! Why are you so jumpy?"

"You scared the mess out of me and you almost got kicked. Did you knock before you barged in my room?" Makenzie shouted. She rolled her eyes as she pulled the earplugs from her ears and sat up straight.

"I knocked twice but you didn't answer and now I see

why. I told you about listening to that iPod so loud. You're going to go deaf one day," Ms. Pierce fussed.

"Seriously mom, what is it now?"

Makenzie was annoyed with her mother. She was always coming in her room unannounced. She hated her mother had the lock removed from her bedroom door last year when she caught her ex-boyfriend sneaking out of her room one evening. Makenzie could have sworn she heard her mother snoring when she walked past her room a few moments before, pretending to use the bathroom.

"I came to tell you that your father called to apologize for missing your court appearance. He was called into work and couldn't get out of it," Rhonda softly spoke as she sat on the edge of the bed.

Makenzie laid back and turned on her side with her back to her mother. She did not want to see her father anyway. He only came around once in a while and that was usually when her mother called to tell him Makenzie had done something wrong or to bring her some money. They were once very close but he left her and her mom when she was twelve and their relationship hadn't been the same since.

"Pumpkin, I know you're still mad at your dad for leaving. But, he's trying and you need to learn how to forgive. Let go of the past. You guys use to be so close. You did everything together," Rhonda smiled and patted Makenzie on the back.

A tear ran down Makenzie's cheek. She remembered all the good times she had with her dad. He taught her how to swim at seven years old and how to ride a bike with no training wheels when she was only five. He even taught her to play the piano, something she hadn't touched since he left. She missed those days but he betrayed her and she didn't think she could ever forgive him.

You Got Me Twisted

"Remember that time when you, your dad and Kalvin went--"

"Mom!" Makenzie shouted. "Get out of my room!"

"What is wrong with you? You don't have to yell," Rhonda said as she stood to her feet and walked out the door.

Makenzie's mother knew her daughter took her dad's departure hard. She became a different child when he left. Her once sweet, spunky personality was now hostile and short-tempered. She yelled and talked back almost daily. Rhonda Pierce knew she let Makenzie go way too far sometimes. Yelling, cussing and even name calling happened more often than she would have liked.

The disrespect didn't start until after her ex-husband Walter left them. Rhonda knew how much pain her daughter was in so she allowed her to take it out on her, hoping it would soon pass. But, here they were four years later and things had gotten worse.

Rhonda felt part to blame for the pain Makenzie was going through. She felt that if she had been a better wife maybe he wouldn't have left. When Walter moved out she didn't understand why. She was happily married and assumed he was too. They rarely even argued so the separation was a total shock to her. She beat herself up every day trying to figure out where she went wrong and silently carried the guilt of her failed marriage around for years.

Makenzie was a mute for weeks when her father first moved. Rhonda tried taking her for counseling but she refused to talk. After three weeks of no progress, she discontinued the sessions. The following week, Rhonda was walking past Makenzie's room when she heard laughter. She slowly pushed the door open and found her looking at an old episode of Moesha. Rhonda wanted to cry with joy but held her tears back, sat down next to her daughter and laughed along with her. From that day forward she couldn't get Makenzie to stop talking. She wasn't sure why she suddenly started speaking again. The only thing she could come up with was that her prayers had finally been answered.

Makenzie was glad her mother left her room when she did. She didn't think she could hold in the river of tears fighting to escape her eyes another second. Hearing the name Kalvin after all this time made her skin feel like a thousand bugs were crawling all over her body.

chapter 4

akenzie's summer break was over just when it was starting to get exciting. A month had passed since the incident with Jordan and although he pissed her off about the whole Shayla thing, she was willing to forgive him had he called to apologize. But, after a leaving several messages, giving him the opportunity to ask her for forgiveness, she had finally given up.

Hanging out with her girl Mya helped her to get past Jordan. They had plans for some type of adventure every other day. If they weren't shopping at the mall they were swimming at the beach or kicking it at somebody's party.

School would be starting in a week and Makenzie knew her days of staying up until all hours of the night and rising late the next morning would soon come to an end. Her school schedule would be hectic as always; five classes, track practice and weekly meetings with the newspaper committee.

Today, school was the last thing on Makenzie's mind. She and Mya were meeting up with friends at the 10 Pins Bowling alley in downtown Chicago in a few hours and she had to look *fly*. She was crushing on Issayah Miller and heard that he would be there. She ran into him four times in the last two weeks and felt fate was in the mix. They both attended the same parties and shared a few mutual friends. She knew he was checking for her too. His boy Chris let Mya know that Issayah was feeling her and there was no way Mya was going to keep that information from her girl.

Makenzie heard her cellular phone vibrate against the top of her nightstand. She leaped across her bed to grab it. She predicted it was Mya checking to see if she was ready to go. She picked up her Blackberry and pressed the text mail icon.

Mya: R u ready?

Makenzie: Almost. I need a few more minutes.

Mya: U hav 20 mins b4 I get there so b in front of the house.

Makenzie: K

Makenzie jumped in and out the shower in ten minutes, slid into her blue jean shorts, emerald tank top and matching flip flops. Next, she brushed her teeth and bumped a few curls in her hair.

Honk. Honk.

Makenzie ran out the door with her jumbo emerald hoop earrings in hand, slamming the door behind her. She hopped in the passenger side of Mya's red, Volkswagen Jetta.

"I told you to be outside, slow one," Mya joked as she drove west on Sibley Boulevard.

"I believe I still had two minutes left, thank you very much," Makenzie said as she pulled down the visor to view herself in the small mirror. She placed her earrings in her ears and applied a fresh coat of her new lip gloss she picked up from the beauty supply store the day before.

Makenzie couldn't believe how close she and Mya had become. When she first met her, she thought Mya was kind of weird. It was their first meeting for Blue News, the school paper at Thorncrest High and she was dressed in a black bubble skirt, black and white polka dot leggings, a yellow t-shirt with peace symbols all over it and Converse gym shoes that stopped right below her knees. Her hair was shaved in a medium length Mohawk and dyed a bright red. She had four holes in each ear and one in her left eyebrow. But, once she looked past all that and really got to know her, she was the realist girl she'd met at the school.

Driving downtown in Chicago was a no-no. The traffic was always crazy busy and the parking rates where off the chart. They had five minutes to pull into a parking space and race up the Metra stairs to the platform before the train arrived. They jumped out the car and sped through the lot. Mya folded a dollar bill, located her parking spot number on the payment box then slid it inside then ran through the viaduct to the stairwell as fast as they could.

"Mya, come on girl! The train is pulling in," Makenzie yelled from the top of the staircase.

"I'm coming, just hold the door," Mya said as she jogged up the last few steps struggling to breathe.

"You almost made us miss the train," Makenzie said as they entered the train's vestibule.

"Well, everyone can't be a track star like you," Mya said, taking a window seat in the center of the train.

"Yeah, I guess you're right. I am a track star," she smiled.

"Whatever, bighead."

"So what's up with you and Chris? Makenzie asked Mya.

"Where did that come from? And, what do you mean what's up? Chris is cool but he's not my type. You're not thinking about Chris anyway. What you really want to know is if Issayah's going to be there," Mya answered while texting simultaneously.

"Yeah, you're right," they laughed. "But still, what's wrong with Chris? He's cute, he's a baller and he's popular," Makenzie said as her eyebrows moved closer to her hairline.

"Exactly!"

Gloria Dotson-Lewis

"What? I don't get it," Makenzie laughed.

"Do you know how many females like Chris at school? I'd probably have to fight someone every week for trying to come at him. No thank you," Mya shook her head.

"Yep, you're right. Those chicks are thirsty. They have no respect for relationships up there. They'll come at your man in a minute. There's a fight at least once a month over some dude. It's crazy."

"Right, and I ain't down for that type of drama so you may as well leave that subject alone. Guess who I drove past on the way to pick you up," Mya changed the topic.

"Who?"

"Jordan."

"For real? Where did you see him?"

"He was turning in the Walgreens parking lot in Dolton."

"Umm . . . who cares? I'm so over him. I'm checking for Issayah now," Makenzie smiled.

"I'm glad you're done with him. He had you snapping. The whole court situation was a mess by itself but then you go over his crib and get into it with him and some female. Girl, you lucky you didn't go back to jail that day," Mya shook her head.

"I was going over there to talk and see if we could work things out. When I saw ole girl I lost it. She started talking smack so I had to give her the business. You know how I get when my buttons are pressed."

"True that. Oh, the next stop is ours," Mya said as she placed her cell phone in her front pocket and headed towards the exit.

The sun beamed on downtown Chicago as the train pulled into its final stop. The John Hancock, Trump Tower and Willis Tower which is the tallest building in the United States, helped to give Chicago one of the best skylines in the world. The busy streets, lined with plenty of restaurants, theatres and stores, were filled with residents and tourists enjoying the eighty degree weather as they strolled down the sidewalks.

The smell of dew from the nearby Chicago River filled the air as Makenzie and Mya headed north on the Magnificent Mile. Their destination was only a half mile away but it took them longer than normal to get there as they window shopped at Forever 21 and the Gap before heading west on Ohio Street.

The bowling alley was packed but Mya quickly spotted their friends on the opposite side of the room. She grabbed Makenzie's arm and walked pass the circular bar. Bowling balls rolled down neon lit lanes as a Kanye West and Jay Z's video played on the huge screens mounted on the foot of each lane.

"What up? It's about time ya'll got here. We're on our second game," Chris said as he stood up to give them each a hug.

"My brother was late getting back with my car. We had to wait another hour for the next train," Mya explained as she looked at the scores. "I see you're getting your butt kicked."

"It ain't over. Haven't you heard of a come back? I do it all the time at my games."

"That's basketball, this is bowling."

"It don't matter, basketball, bowling ball, I can master them all."

"You're so . . . "

"Confident."

"More like cocky."

Makenzie laughed inside as she noticed Chris checking out Mya. She used to believe he was looking at her like she

19

was an alien walking the face of the earth in her over the top outfits. But, as she paid closer attention, she knew he liked what he saw. Mya's baby bottom bronze skin was naturally pretty and had no need for make-up. She had on a pair of denim shorts with orange leggings underneath that looked like someone had cut them up with a razor, a red t-shirt that read "Don't Act Like You're Not Impressed" on the front and a pair of shoes that one would wear to a tap dancing performance. Chris checked her out up, down and sideways. Makenzie was tripping so hard on Chris that she didn't even notice Issayah walk up.

"Hey Makenzie, I started to think Chris was lying about ya'll coming up here," Issayah said right before taking a sip of the bottled water he was holding.

"Umm, I know you see more than Makenzie, Issayah," Maya said with her lips twisted and her hands on her hips.

"It ain't even like that. I thought you and Chris was in the middle of a conversation. You know I was gone speak to you girl."

"Huh, I don't know. I think when my girl steps in the room you don't see nobody else."

"Shut up Mya," Makenzie said blushing with embarrassment.

"I'm just saying." Mya hunched her shoulders.

"Come on girl," Chris said grabbing Mya's hand, directing her to a seat in front of lane eleven where six other friends were waiting.

Issayah walked with Makenzie to rent some bowling shoes. He stood five inches over her 5'3" petite frame. His ebony smooth skin and perfect pearly white teeth was what initially attracted Makenzie to him but his conversation is what kept her interested. She couldn't stand a guy whose conversation was limited to sex, rap and sports. But,

Makenzie was surprised he hadn't asked for her number yet. He didn't appear to be shy and her intuition was telling her that he was feeling her.

"You look really nice today," Issayah complemented.

"Today? Does that mean I usually look a mess?" Makenzie joked.

"I don't think you could look a mess even if you tried."

"Wow, now that's the best line I've ever heard," Makenzie giggled.

"Naw shorty, I'm serious. You look good every time I see you," Issayah said as they reached the shoe rental counter.

She looked at him and smiled. "Thanks."

Makenzie grabbed the size six worn shoes from the blond haired, pale lady behind the counter. They headed back to their friends and played two more games before leaving for Grand Lux Café to eat. The host directed them to a booth table with a window overlooking the strip after their thirty minute wait.

They agreed to split up in groups so their wait wouldn't be as long. Chris, Mya, Issayah and Makenzie sat together while their other friends sat at another table.

"Have you been here before?" Makenzie asked Issayah who sat next to her looking over the menu.

"Naw, but I heard the food is good."

"Yes! The food is on point. I've been here at least three times and I haven't tasted anything I don't like yet."

"Me either," Mya agreed, sitting across from Makenzie.

"I don't know what to order so I'm going to let you order for me since you know the menu so well," Issayah said, closing his menu.

"Are you for real?" Makenzie smiled at him.

"Yeah, I trust you."

"Okay dude, Makenzie may order you something crazy

like octopus. Then you'll have to sit over there and pretend you like it just to impress her," Chris laughed.

"That would be too funny," Mya said.

"Anyway," Makenzie rolled her eyes at them. "Is there anything you don't like?"

"I don't do pork and I'm allergic to shell fish but other than that I pretty much eat anything."

"Cool. I'm going to order you the crispy caramel chicken and I'll get the fettuccini alfredo with chicken. They're both really good and they give you really big portions here. We can share, that way you'll get a chance to taste two different entrees."

"Awww, ain't that cute? They're going to share each other's food," Mya teased.

"Don't worry about the haters across the table Makenzie," Issayah joked.

"What haters? I don't see anyone," she laughed, playing along.

"Oh, it's like that?" Mya said as the waitress walked up to take their order.

The quad sat at the table for over an hour eating and enjoying each other's company. The couple next to them gave them nasty glances for laughing so loud. Makenzie and Mya excused themselves to use the restroom right after finishing their meals while the guys took care of the bill.

"Mya, girl, I am so feeling Issayah," she said as she placed her hand under the touchless soap dispenser.

"He's definitely feeling you too. I couldn't believe it when he wiped that pasta sauce off your face. You guys are acting like a real couple and haven't even exchanged numbers yet.

"I couldn't believe it either but I thought that was so sweet. He did finally ask for my number when we walked over here from 10 Pins. And, on top of that he paid for my food. Issayah Miller gets an A for today," Makenzie stated as she smoothed down the sides of her ponytail with her hands. "I may even let him take me on prom."

"Whoa, don't you think that's a little premature?" Mya said. "That's next year." Mya stopped combing her hair as she eyeballed Makenzie's reflection in the mirror.

"Maybe, but I just have a good feeling about this one," she smiled.

The girls walked back towards their table laughing at Makenzie's future prediction. The restaurant's décor was upscale with its marble floors, European painted wall designs and slightly dimmed lighting. Voices and laughter filled the packed room as waiters and waitresses quickly moved about.

As they neared the table, Makenzie slowed her stride. Her inner eyebrows lowered and her heart slightly raced as she saw a fair skinned girl with shoulder length hair hugging Issayah. He told her he didn't have a girlfriend so Makenzie wanted to know who this chick was hugging on her future boo.

"Excuse me," Makenzie said with an attitude as she squeezed past the girl in the yellow sundress and matching flip-flops.

"Makenzie and Mya, this is Robyn and her girl Kelly. Robyn and I are on the Drama Team together," Issayah said.

"Hi," Mya said. "I've seen you around school a few times."

"Yeah, you do look familiar," Robyn smiled. "I think I've seen you before to," she said looking at Makenzie.

"Sorry, I can't say the same," Makenzie dryly answered.

She couldn't believe that Mya was conversing with them. She saw how Robyn was smiling all in Issayah's face and she didn't like it. She was boiling inside and wanted to punch her in the face.

"Mya, what time does the next train leave?" Makenzie asked cutting off their conversation.

"Let me check the schedule." Mya unzipped her purse and searched around for the Metra booklet.

"I wanted to try some of the pineapple upside-down cake and ice cream. You sure you can't stay a little longer?" Issayah asked looking down at Makenzie.

She really enjoyed their unexpected date and really wanted to say yes but was feeling disrespected by Robyn's presence. She thought Issayah should have sent Robyn and her girl on their way when she and Mya came back from the washroom not stand around laughing and joking with them while ignoring her.

"Naw, I suddenly lost my appetite," Makenzie said as she slid out the booth seat. "Maybe I'll holla at you later. Let's go Mya."

chapter 5

*I*t was Saturday morning and Makenzie thought of a million and one other things she could be doing. She didn't agree with this whole therapy thing and wish she could get up and walk out. But, since it was ordered by the court, she had no choice but to stay.

Today would be her third session and she had yet to discuss anything significant. They made small talk about movies, music and fashion. She just didn't see the purpose of talking to a stranger about her personal business.

Makenzie thought Dr. Reid was pretty cool. She was young, maybe in her early thirties, her hair was always together and she wore the flyist clothes. She didn't talk down to her like some know it all adults but really seemed to listen to what she had to say, although that wasn't much. Makenzie didn't feel she needed any help. If people would just stop pushing her buttons, she wouldn't have to snap on them.

The brightly lit small waiting area was painted a burnt orange and was set off with chocolate brown leather furniture. The soft paintings and hardwood floors gave a relaxing spa feel. Rhonda Pierce sat on the opposite end of the couch looking through an *Essence* magazine while Makenzie texted several of her friends simultaneously. They both looked up when the office door opened.

"Good morning, ladies. Sorry to keep you waiting. Makenzie, you can come on back," Dr. Reid said as she held the door open.

Makenzie flopped down on a couch and continued texting.

"Makenzie, can you turn off your phone while we're in session please?" Dr. Reid sat in a chair across from Makenzie with a pad and pen on her lap.

"I'm really hoping we can talk this week. I'd like to get to know a little bit more about you. What school do you attend?"

"Thorncrest."

"Really! I graduated from Thorncrest but that was fifteen years ago," she chuckled. "Is Mrs. Tally still there? "

"Yep, she's still there. She needs to retire though. She misplaces our work sometimes then makes us do it over," Makenzie said twisting her lips.

"Oh wow, that is something," Dr. Reid chuckled.

"Do you like school?"

"It's okay I guess," she hunched her shoulders.

"Well, can you tell me what your favorite pastime is?"

"I don't have one," Makenzie said dryly as she slouched down on the couch.

"Everyone likes to do something. Do you participate on any teams or clubs at school?"

"I'm on the track team and the school newspaper."

"Ok. Are you pretty fast?" Dr. Reid smiled. She was glad that Makenzie had finally opened up about something. The first two sessions she couldn't get her to talk about herself so she discussed general topics with her to warm her up. But, at the end of their last meeting, Dr. Reid reminded her that it would be in her best interest to talk to her since she would have to report her progress to the judge.

"I came in first place last year in the 400 meter dash when we went to state," Makenzie said.

"Wow, that's great Makenzie. You must be proud."

"Yeah, it was one of the best moments of my life. There were some really fast girls from those other schools. To go to state and bring the trophy back was great," she said as she sat up on the couch.

"You also mentioned you're on the school paper. That sounds really interesting."

"It is. I really enjoy writing and getting feedback from other students."

"Do you have a lot of friends at school?"

"Just a few. Too many friends bring drama and I don't get down like that. The girls are either jealous of you or think you want their man. The guys either want to get in your panties or they're spreading rumors that they got em' already."

"Has that ever happened to you?" Dr. Reid enquired.

"What? You mean has anyone spread rumors about me?" Makenzie pointed to herself. "Never. I don't play like that. It would be on if someone tried to put me out there like that. I'm not one of those weak girls that let guys run over her," she said as her neck moved in every direction imaginable.

"Is that what Jordan Davis was trying to do? Run over you?

"Jordan could never run over me. I can't stand when females let guys push them around and control them. That will never happen to me again," Makenzie rolled her eyes, leaned back against the couch and crossed her arms.

"Again? Did someone do something to hurt you before."

Makenzie moved around uncomfortably in her seat then shook her head no. She was getting really irritated that Dr. Reid was trying to get all in her business.

"Ok, Well, can you tell me what happened the day you sprayed painted Jordan's car?"

"It's complicated and it's a long story."

"I'm all ears."

Makenzie looked at her cell phone to check the time. She had fifteen minutes left to get through this session. There was no way she was going to stay and answer another question.

"Sorry doc, I don't feel so good. I need to go home and lay down." She got up and walked out, slamming the office door behind her.

chapter 6

Makenzie sat on the stairs of her front porch texting Mya as she waited on Issayah to scoop her up. They were going to Hollywood Park in Crestwood to hang out. She was really feeling him and was looking forward to their first date alone together. Both their schedules were usually crazy busy so they had to find time to even talk on the phone some days. Issayah had Drama practice every day after school plus he worked at WalMart part time. The school newspaper and the track team kept Makenzie pretty business on top of her school work.

She chose to wear some fitted, stretch, faded jeans with a red Puma t-shirt and spotless white Puma gym shoes. Makenzie aimed at being cute but she also wanted to be comfortable. She was very competitive and planned on kicking Issayah's butt in every game they played today. She recently had extensions added to her hair. It was pulled back into an underhand French braid that laid neatly down the center of her back. A thin layer of eyeliner was neatly drawn across her upper eyelid and lilac lip gloss shimmered on her full lips.

Makenzie smiled when she spotted Issayah pulling up in his mother's white Ford Equinox. He smiled back showing off his perfectly white Crest commercial teeth. She walked around to the passenger side, got inside and reached over to hug him before strapping herself in.

"So are you ready to get smashed in some Skeeball and miniature golf?" Issayah asked.

"What? Please. You must not have a clue of who you're messing with. I am skee ball queen. They even have my picture on the wall up there," Makenzie joked.

"Is that right? We'll see. Just don't expect me to go easy on you cause you're fine. I play to win," Issayah said as he turned onto Cicero.

Makenzie blushed at Issayah's comment. He was always throwing compliments her way and she caught every one of them.

"You talk a whole lot of mess. I hope you can back it up," Makenzie playfully rolled her eyes.

It was a Thursday evening. The parking lot was fairly empty compared to a Friday or Saturday when Makenzie usually visited. Issayah pulled in a parking spot and turned off the engine. They exited the car and met at the rear. He embraced Makenzie around the neck as they walked towards the entrance. Her heart did a race up her throat and back to her chest from the touch of his arm against her skin.

"Can I have a good luck kiss?" Issayah whispered in her ear.

"I'll give you a kiss but it won't be for good luck," Makenzie said before tilting her head back into the pit of his arm.

"I'll take that," he said before leaning down to kiss Makenzie on the lips.

Issayah's lips were warmer and softer than any boy she had ever kissed before. It was only a three second peck but Makenzie could swear she felt an electrical shock shoot through her body. She wanted him to kiss her again but she didn't want him to know how much she enjoyed it. She heard her cousin Malkomb and his friends dogging out girls who would sweat them. They liked the females who gave them a challenge not the easy ones.

You Got Me Twisted

The oversized, miniature golf course located on both sides of the building, expanded around the rear. Makenzie and Issayah walked up the wheelchair accessible ramp and entered through the double doors. Two statues, of the old rap group the Beastie Boys, sat just left of the entrance. The brightly lit room was filled with multiple sounds, from video games to chattering children. The smell of nachos filled the space which made Makenzie's stomach roar like a hungry lion.

Issayah guided Makenzie over to the massive prize center to the right. Small prizes laid neatly positioned in the glass counter while large stuffed animals hung from the wall behind it. A freckled face teenage boy with red hair was assisting a little girl in front of them with choosing her toy. They had to purchase their game cards before they could get started. A couple of minutes later, Issayah handed the attendant a twenty dollar bill for their game card and they headed towards the back to play skee ball first.

"You ready to get this butt whooping," Issayah said as he slid the card in his machine and then Makenzie's.

"Let's do this!" Makenzie said as she picked up one of the brown wooden balls and attempted to roll it.

"Hold up sexy. There are some extra rules to this game," Issayah said as he gently grabbed Makenzie's arm.

There goes another compliment.

"Extra rules? So, you're about to start cheating already?" Makenzie said, putting her hands on her hips.

"I never cheat. I just want to make it a little more interesting."

"Okay… let's hear this," Makenzie hesitantly responded.

"This is going to be like the NBA Playoffs, the best four out of seven, wins. "

"That's cool. I ain't scared. And the winner gets what?"

31

"The loser has to tell the winner three things she likes about him."

"You mean the loser has to tell her three things he likes about her?"

Issayah laughed. "Let's do this," he said before leaning over and kissing Makenzie on the lips again.

They rolled their balls up the ramp and into the holes trying to score as many points as they could. They spent the next ten minutes talking trash as they took turns bragging about their wins. Issayah won the first two games, Makenzie the next three and then Issayah game back to tie it up. It was down to same seven. Makenzie aimed several times to hit the fifty point slot but only successfully made it in once. She glanced over at Issayah's score. He had her beat by fifty-five points. She only had one ball left and the only chance she had to win was to go for the one hundred points, which was on the top right-hand corner and almost impossible to hit. She held the ball in her hand and concentrated on her target.

"Come on, give it up. Maybe you'll win something else," Issayah teased.

Makenzie ignored him. She rolled the ball hitting the top corner of her target. It bounced up and then went straight in. She couldn't believe her luck. She jumped up and down shouting 'yes'.

"Now what, loser," Makenzie said as she threw up her right index finger and thumb to form the letter 'L'.

"Ok, you got lucky. It's cool. What you wanna do next?" Issayah said as he glanced around the room.

"Before we do anything I need to eat something. My stomach is making all kinds of sounds. And while we're eating, you can tell me the three things you like about me," Makenzie snickered.

"I see you're going to rub this loss in my face all day."

"Yeah, pretty much."

"That's what I thought," Issayah said, shaking his head.

They headed to the food counter and ordered their food. Makenzie got the nachos topped with ground beef, extra cheese and extra peppers. Issayah purchased the Philly cheese-steak, fries and a Sprite. They grabbed their food, found a table in the dining area and sat across from each other.

"So, let's hear it," Makenzie looked over at Issayah.

"Hear what?"

"Quit playing. You lost so pay up. Unless…you really don't like me and have nothing to say," Makenzie said before popping another nacho chip in her mouth.

"What? I know you don't believe that. Why would I waste my time hanging out with you if I didn't like you?"

Makenzie hunched her shoulders. "People do crazy things everyday."

"I ain't gone lie, I'm really feeling you. First of all, man, you're fine. I like your style. You're hair and gear is always on point. You don't where all that make up. You're just natural. Another reason why I like you is you're fun to hang out with. You don't act all shy and boring. And today I discovered that I like those soft lips of yours."

Makenzie could not hold back her smile. Her body suddenly felt warm and fuzzy. She could not believe how sweet he was. Guys usually played their feelings cool but he wasn't afraid to express himself. Makenzie scooted out of her booth seat and sat next to Issayah.

"Awwe, that was so sweet," She said, before kissing him on the lips.

"Are you making fun of me?" Issayah pulled his neck back and looked in her eyes.

"No! I'm serious. That was really sweet. I actually like

you for all the same reasons. I also like the fact that you're not afraid to express your feelings which you've just proven. Most guys think it's weak."

"What you'll find out about me is I'm not most guys. I'm just gone do me. I don't worry about what other folks think. People always gone have something to say about you anyway. I like you and I want you to know it. What's so weak about that?"

"Nothing, I'm liking it," Makenzie smiled.

"Then that's all that matters."

They finished up their food then proceeded to ride the go carts and bumper cars, play some miniature golf then finished up with rock climbing. They were laughing at Makenzie's first experience at climbing the twenty-seven foot wall. Heights had always been one of her biggest fears so every time she came to Hollywood Park, she would just watch her friends climb. But, Issayah convinced her she would be fine and he'd be right by her side the whole way up. He made her feel safe so she went for it. She was nervous the whole time but once they were back on the ground, she was ecstatic and couldn't wait to tell Mya.

"Did you have fun?" Issayah asked Makenzie on their ride home.

"Are you kidding? I beat you in skee ball and miniature golf. I had a great time," Makenzie giggled.

"Here you go," Issayah said, shaking his head. "Let's not forget, I beat you in go-cart racing and air hockey. I would say we're even."

"You cheated in air hockey. I was not ready when you hit that puck on the last round. So, you're not getting credit for that."

"Huh, don't tell me you're a sore loser," Issayah commented, as he pulled in front of Makenzie's house.

"Never, I'm just calling it what it is."

"Ok, Imma let you have that. Can I get a kiss before you go in the house?"

Makenzie leaned towards him without saying a word. Issayah, gently took her face in his hands and kissed her freshly glossed lips. He parted her mouth with his tongue to deepen their affection. Makenzie closed her eyes and enjoyed the moment. It felt so good and she didn't want it to end.

Bam . . . Bam . . . Bam

"Makenzie, who is this? Get your hands off her!" A masculine voice shouted.

Makenzie and Issayah were startled by the commotion. They immediately separated and glanced in the direction of the banging. When Makenzie looked up she cringed and instantly became nauseous. She couldn't believe this was happening after such a perfect date. She opened her door and hopped out.

"Omg, I'm so sorry," she said to Issayah right before she slammed the door shut and ran towards the house.

Gloria Dotson-Lewis

chapter 7

Rhonda woke Makenzie up at 7 a.m. every Saturday morning so they could clean, wash and shop. Makenzie felt like slapping her mother every time she came in her room, pumped up on caffeine, shouting rise and shine in her ear. While most normal people took advantage of the weekend by sleeping late, they were wide awake wiping down walls and dusting window sills as old dusties blared from the living room speakers.

This Saturday her mother didn't have to wake her, Issayah's early morning call beat her to it. He had to work then attend a rehearsal for a school play and this was the only time he would be able to talk to her until late this evening.

"Hello," Makenzie said groggily into the receiver.

"Hey cutie, did I wake you?"

"Yeah, but it's okay. Do you always get up this early on the weekend?"

"Naw, only when I have to work. I called you yesterday but I didn't get answer. You told me you had a good time on our date but then you ignore a brother's call. What's up with that?" Issayah said in a playful tone.

"I would say I didn't hear it but I'd be lying. I really enjoyed our date but I was super embarrassed when you dropped me off," Makenzie said as she nervously bit the index nail on her right hand.

"You don't have to be embarrassed, ma. It's cool. Was that your old man?"

"Yes, unfortunately. He's a drunk as you saw for

yourself. I couldn't believe he was beating on your window like that."

"I didn't know what was going on. He banged on the window like he was the police or something," Issayah joked.

"I know, right. That was crazy."

"Well, we all have dysfunctional peeps. My dad left my moms when I was only two so I know about deadbeats. I know one thing though, I'll never be like him. Imma take care of my shorties."

"Makenzie," Makenzie heard her mother shout from down stairs.

"Huhhh, my mother's calling me. I need to get ready to go to the store so let me get off this phone. Text me later if you can."

"Ok, beautiful."

"Ok."

Makenzie quickly showered and got dressed. Rhonda didn't like to get caught up in the crowds so they got up, dressed and headed to Ultra Foods in Lansing to beat the morning rush. She was always prepared with a list and knew where to find everything in the store. She'd been shopping at Ultra for over ten years and had gotten to know some of the employees personally.

They pulled into a spot not far from the entrance. As they walked through the automatic double doors Makenzie grabbed a shopping cart from the right of the vestibule then proceeded through a second set of double doors. Lays Potato Chips were stacked on a rack, on sale two for $5.00. Makenzie snagged a bag of Flamin' Hot and Dill Pickle flavored chips and tossed them in the cart.

"Makenzie, put one of those back. I'm only getting what's on my list," Rhonda commanded.

"But, I like them both and they're only $5.00 so what's

the big deal," Makenzie rolled her eyes behind her mother's back.

"Do you have anything on the groceries today? If not, put one of them back."

"Whatever," Makenzie huffed as she threw the Dill Pickle chips back.

Makenzie texted Mya while slowly pushing the buggy behind her mother. The only shopping she enjoyed was for clothes and shoes. She didn't see why her mother couldn't come to the store by herself anyway. She could've been home catching up on the DVR recorded episode of the Bad Girls Club she missed last week.

"Mom, remember I told you that Mya and I are going to Fright Fest at Great America this year? Well, I need money so I can buy my ticket and costume."

Rhonda picked up a head of lettuce and put it in the cart then checked the item off her list.

"Mom, are you listening to me? I need some money for Great America."

"Makenzie, I don't have money for Great America. I have to buy this food and pay some bills."

"Seriously? What about the money you get from my dad for child support every week? And, isn't that a new purse you're carrying?" Makenzie stopped the cart and pointed to the Gucci purse dangling from her mother's shoulder.

"First of all, what I buy with my money is my business little girl. And secondly, that child support is sent to me to help pay for everything you have like a roof over your head, heat, electricity, food--"

"Okay, okay, I get it, deg."

"Call your dad and ask him," Makenzie's mom said as she placed two plum tomatoes in a plastic bag.

Makenzie rolled her eyes. "How about you ask him for

me? I don't want to be bothered."

"Nope, I'm not getting in it. If you want it bad enough then you call him yourself, otherwise don't go."

"Whatever," Makenzie popped her lips.

She knew her father would give her the money but she didn't feel up to pretending that she liked him. He always wanted to sit and talk before he coughed up the dough and it took everything in her power to be nice. She would rather be tossed in a sea full of sharks then have him sit up in her face like everything was cool. But, she had to do what she had to do. He was her walking ATM and she needed cash like yesterday.

Rhonda headed to the meat department next, then on to dairy and lastly to pick up her bread which was near the front of the store. After she finished getting all the items from her list they headed for check out. There were two people in front of them, one with groceries filled to the rim. Once they made their way to the front, Rhonda placed the groceries on the conveyer belt then pulled her Chase debit card from her purse. The cashier rang up each item as Makenzie bagged them.

They loaded the food in the trunk and drove home. After Makenzie helped her mother put the groceries up she had to clean her room, both bathrooms and the living room while her mother took care of the kitchen, the dining room and the washing. At 11 a.m. she was finished with her chores and was ready to get into something.

Her boo, Issayah was the first person who popped in her head but he wasn't available so she called her girl Mya.

"Hello."

"Hey Mya, Mya, what you up to?" Makenzie asked.

"Girl, my mother has me cleaning out my closet. Our church is having a clothing give away this weekend and she wants me to give away stuff I don't wear anymore. I'm almost through so what's up?" Mya said as she folded a red t-shirt she hadn't worn in over a year.

"I see your mother is working you to death to. I need to get out this darn house."

"Girl, me too. Where you wanna go?"

"I really don't care. The longer I stay around here, the sooner my mother is going to have me cleaning something else."

"Well I'm hungry. Let's hit Buffalo Wild Wings and then the mall."

"I'm busted and my mother is acting like she don't have no money so I need to call my father. I'll call you when I'm on my way."

"Okay."

Makenzie hung up the phone and dialed her father's cellular phone number. She had his number saved in her contacts as sperm donor. After two rings he answered the call.

"Hey baby girl, how are you?"

"I'm good," Makenzie said as she rolled her eyes in the back of her head as far as they could go. "I need some money. Can I get $100?"

"I just gave you $50 last week. Did you spend that already?"

"Yeah, I told you that was for the new track uniform. Do you have it or not?" Makenzie said, getting irritated. She didn't like him questioning her about the money he gave her and she refused to kiss his butt. Either he would give it to her or he wouldn't.

"Yeah, let me stop at the bank and I'll be right over," Walter answered.

"Okay, well please hurry. I have some place to be."

"Okay, baby girl."

Makenzie hung up without saying goodbye. She cringed every time he called her baby girl. She hoped he got the hint that she didn't have time to sit around talking. She needed him to hand over the cash and be out, nothing more, nothing less.

Makenzie overheard her mother talking on the phone once about how much money her father made working for Northwestern Memorial Hospital as an Environmental Engineer. He made big bucks and Makenzie knew he had plenty to spare. He lived with his mother and drove the same old Maxima he had since 2008 which probably meant no mortgage and no car note.

Makenzie showered then flat ironed her hair. She threw on some skinny Levi jeans with a rose colored stripped sweater that stopped at her waist then placed pearl studs in her ears and a long pearl necklace around her neck. She heard the doorbell ring then ten seconds later, her mother calling her name.

"Makenzie."

"I heard you the first time," Makenzie said as she descended the stairs.

"Well, I have washing to finish. Tell your mom I said hello," Rhonda said to her ex-husband before exiting the living room.

"Sure thing," he smiled.

Everyone always told Makenzie she looked just like her father but she didn't see it. They both had the same golden bronze skin tone and almond shaped eyes. No doubt her father had potential to be a very handsome man but the smell of alcohol that was coming from his body made him the ugliest man in the world to her right now. He raised his arms and stepped towards Makenzie.

"Umm, do you have the money?" Makenzie said as she stepped back.

"You can't give your old man a hug?"

As much as she didn't want to hug him, she knew he would start asking why and that would just prolong his visit. She leaned in, rapped her arms around his neck, gave him a quick pat on the back and released him.

"How is school going? You're a Freshmen right?" He asked as he stumbled towards the couch and flopped down.

"A sophomore," she said as she rolled her eyes.

"That's right, a sophomore. When is your next track meet? I wanna see my baby run."

"I don't have my schedule but I'll call and let you know," Makenzie lied. There was no way she would allow him to show up at one of her competitions drunk and embarrass her in front of everyone. She didn't want him to step foot near her school or near any of her friends for that matter.

"Maybe we can hang out next weekend. I'll cook your favorite meal if you come to the house," Walter said.

"I think I'm busy with school stuff for the next month but I'll let you know. My friend is waiting for me to pick her up. I need to finish getting ready but I'll call you tomorrow or something," Makenzie said as she moved towards the front door.

"You never have time for your pops. I still love you though."

He struggled to get up from the couch, falling back down twice before finally getting to his feet. His eyes were half closed and his words slurred together as he talked. Makenzie couldn't understand much of what he was saying; then again she wasn't trying to hear him anyway.

"Can I get a hug before I go?"

Makenzie gave him a quick embrace then opened the

door. She threw her arm across the doorway as he proceeded to leave.

"Aren't you forgetting something," she said with her hand out.

"Oh yeah, the money," he chuckled. "How much do you need again?"

"A hundred and fifty," she said without flinching.

He pulled a wad of money from his pocket and handed Makenzie eight, twenty dollar bills. She smiled at the extra sixty dollars.

"Thanks, I'll call you tomorrow," she said as she placed a hand in the center of his back, slowly pushed him out the door, then shut it behind him.

"Or not," she said as she rolled her eyes and ran up the stairs.

chapter 8

*U*mmm, look at you Ms. Thang," Mya said to Makenzie as she walked towards the locker they shared. "What you looking all extra cute for today? Oh yeah, ever since you and Issayah started kickin it, you come to school dressed like you have a modeling shoot to go to," Mya giggled at her own joke.

"Haha, very funny. You know I have to stay looking hot for my man. There's too many thirsty tricks up in here that have their eyes on him. I'm trying to make sure his eyes are only on me," Makenzie responded as she put her hands on her hips, crossed one leg in front of the other and slowly twirled around.

She rocked a pair of soft mint green skinny jeans that hugged her size 6 shapely frame and a loose fitted crème top that hung slightly to one side, exposing her right shoulder. Her three and a half inch shoes were mint with a crème sole. Her blinged out oversized earrings, long flowing gold necklace and sparkling bangles gave her outfit that extra pop.

"Whatever. I'm gonna continue doing me and if my man strays to some bootylicious chick like you then he wasn't mines to begin with. You'll never catch me in nobody's stilettos. This right here is me," Mya said as she pointed to her wide, ankle length red and black plaid skirt, short sleeve white ruffled blouse and black cowboy boots.

"Mya, what are you talking about? You don't even

have a man," Makenzie laughed.

"Well, when I do get a man he'll need to be all about Mya," she said as she rolled her eyes at her friend.

"Speaking of . . . hey Chris," Makenzie said to Issayah's bestfriend as he walked towards them.

"What up Makenzie? Hey Mya," Chris said as he slid next to Mya and put his arm around her shoulders.

"Chris, you gone have all these females up here trying to jump me," Mya tilted her head back as she looked up at Chris.

"I wish any of these bust downs would mess with you."

Chris stood a whole foot over Mya. He looked like he could pass for Diggy Simmon's big brother except he was a little darker. Not only was he cute but his swagger was undeniable. He sported a blue and gold Nike warm-up with matching AirMax jumpers that bear his initials, CK, on the tongue.

"Where is my boo?" Makenzie asked.

"Here he comes," Mya pointed.

Issayah swayed up the hall. A gold link chain hung over his black Sean John t-shirt as his skinny True Religion jeans slightly sagged below his waste. His perfectly trimmed mustache and thick eyebrows looked like they were painted on his face. Waves covered his low cut fade and a small diamond stud blinged in his left ear. Issayah looked Makenzie up and down then took her in his arms and gently squeezed her around the waist.

"You look nice baby."

"Awwe, thank you baby." Makenzie rapped her arms around his neck then kissed him on the lips.

"Ya'll need to get a room," Mya frowned.

"I agree. Ya'll think we can go eat now?" Chris fussed.

Gloria Dotson-Lewis

They all shared fifth period lunch. They headed to the cafeteria and sat down at their regular table after getting their food. Makenzie and Issayah sat on one side and Mya and Chris on the other. The smell of burgers, nacho cheese and pizza dominated the air as the chatter and laughter of students filled the large room.

"Have ya'll had Ms. Welch before?" Makenzie asked.

"I had her last year. She should not be teaching Math. I was lost all year long. I learned everything from my tutor," Issayah answered.

"Awe man, I thought it was just me. She moves super fast and will jump to the next chapter before anyone even understands anything. I'm about to pull my hair out in that class and I have her first period too."

"Let me know if you need my help. I got that Trig down pack now."

"For real! Yes! I'll definitely need your help. I'm so lucky to have a man that's cute and smart," Makenzie said then leaned in to give Issayah a kiss.

"So Mya, when you gone let me take you out?" Chris said changing the subject.

"Let's see . . . how about . . . next never," she said before pinching Chris' cheek.

"I'm a nice guy. Why you always giving me such a hard time?"

"Chris please, you got all these girls up here clowning over you. What you want with me?"

"I ain't thinking about these females up here. I'm trying to get with you."

"Yeah Mya, he's trying to get with you," Makenzie chimed in.

"There you go all up in my business."

"You should gone and give my boy a chance," Issayah

46

added. "He's cool people."

"All ya'll get up off me."

"I just want you to be happy like me and my boo," Makenzie said as she got out her seat and sat sideways across Issayah's lap with one arm around his neck.

"You two are way too mushy for me," Mya said as they laughed.

"Hey Issayah."

They all looked up at the same time to see who was speaking. Robyn stood at the head of the table in her blue jean miniskirt and red BCBG t-shirt. Her hair was swooped in a ponytail that rested above her shoulder blades.

"Oh, hey what's up Robyn."

"I'm sorry. Did I interrupt?"

"Well . . ." Makenzie began.

"Naw, it's cool," Issayah jumped in.

"You're Mya and you're Melissa right?" She pointed.

She knows my darn name. There's something about her that just don't sit right with me.

"It's Makenzie . . ." Makenzie stressed as she mean mugged Robyn.

"Oh, my bad. I'm sorry Makenzie . . ." Robyn stressed.

I know darn well she is not mocking me.

"Did you want something?" Makenzie asked with a phony smirk on her face.

"Yes. Issayah, what time are we meeting to practice for the play?"

"Three-thirty in the auditorium like we always do."

"You sure?"

Makenzie looked over at Mya and twisted her lips. She had a strong feeling Robyn liked Issayah and she wanted to cuss her out for stepping to him right in front of her face.

"Girl, you tripping," Issayah said to Robyn.

The bell sounded and students began to clear their tables and head to class. Makenzie stood up and grabbed her small Coach purse and backpack from the chair next to them. Issayah grabbed his and Makenzie's tray while Chris cleared his and Mya's trash from the table and carried it to the garbage can nearby.

"I'll see you guys later. Issayah, I'll see you at practice," Robyn said then switched off.

Makenzie interlocked her arm with Mya as they walked towards the door. "I do not trust that Robyn chick. She likes Issayah," Makenzie whispered.

"I wasn't going to say anything because I know how you get but I was feeling the same way. You walk up to him while his woman is sitting on his lap to ask him a bogus question. Who does that?" Mya said.

"Exactly. She almost got snapped on."

"Well, I'm glad you didn't. Issayah ain't thinking about that girl so don't even trip."

"You're right but all I know is, if she thinks I'm gone let her come between me and my man, she got me twisted."

chapter 9

I should've known," Makenzie laughed when she opened the door for Mya. "Lady GaGa."

"Yep, you know I love me some LG. What better person to go as on Halloween then my girl?"

"They'll probably be hundreds of you walking around Fright Fest tonight."

"True, true. But, the good thing about Lady GaGa is that she has a different style for everyday of the year," Mya said as she admired her costume in Makenzie's full length mirror. The half black, half white imitation leather cat suit clung to her small frame. Its wide shoulders had fake spikes extending out of the sides. Her long white wig, large triangular shaped shades and clunky heals pulled it all together.

"You're right about that but she's just an overrated weirdo to me. Who wears a freakin' meat dress to an awards show?" Makenzie frowned.

"She has her own style and does things by her own terms and that's what I love about her. Folks think I dress weird but I don't care. I don't like following trends, I have my own style."

"Having your own style is one thing, but wearing a meat dress is just crazy. That woman is not from planet earth." Makenzie and Mya laughed.

"Yeah, even I thought that was a bit much," Mya admitted. "I see you're going as a nurse."

"Yep. My father gave me money to buy a costume, but I ended up spending it on those hot True Religion leggings that I showed you online, so I borrowed my aunt's hospital scrubs and one of her lab jackets."

"Who is Issayah going as?"

"Guess?"

"I don't know. Who?"

"A doctor," Makenzie smiled.

"Deg girl, if your smile was any bigger your face would crack."

"Haha, sounds like some hateration is going on up in here."

"Whatever,"

"Issayah is so sweet. I've never dated a guy like him. Most of the guys I've kicked it with act one way around their friends and another way when we're alone. He's feeling me and he doesn't care who knows it. Plus, I've never heard him talk negatively about any female, even when his friends are sitting around dogging some chick out. He's just sexy inside and out."

"How do you know he's not fronting just because you're there?"

"You could be right but something just tells me he's not like that. Whenever we're on the phone and his mother asks him to do something, he never complains. He'll just tell me he'll call me back later. He's close to his mom and talks about her all the time. I guess she's not a pain in the butt like my mom," Makenzie said as she slid on her clogs.

"You're mother is cool. My mom is the pain in the butt," they both laughed.

"What guy do you know who holds the doors open for you and let you order your food first when you go out? I thought it was just his first impression date but he still does it every time. He kind of reminds me of how my father used to be with my mom before he left us. But anyway, that's another subject for another day," Makenzie rolled her eyes.

You Got cMe Twisted

"Sounds like somebody is falling in love," Mya teased.

"I don't know about all that but he's definitely got my full attention. Anyway, what is Mr. Cool Chris wearing tonight?" Makenzie asked.

"He wouldn't tell me. He's acting like its top secret," Mya said twisting her lips. "Are you ready? We need to be heading over to Issayah's to scoop them up. I wanna get to Great America as soon as it gets dark."

"I'm ready," Makenzie said as she grabbed her coat and cell phone off her bed.

Mya drove the three miles from South Holland to Issayah's home in Dolton. As she pulled in front of the house, Makenzie texted him to let them know she and Mya had arrived then moved from the passenger seat to the rear so she and Issayah could sit together.

She and Mya were in the middle of a conversation when the guys walked out. Issayah was dressed like Makenzie in scrubs with a stethoscope hanging around his neck. Chris was dressed in some skinny jeans, a white t-shirt, a waist length red leather jacket with multiple zippers and a large pair of white framed glasses.

Makenzie and Mya tried to guess who he was as the guys approached the car. One said Soulja Boy while the other said Michael Jackson. It wasn't until he got right up to the car when they noticed his jaws looked like a chipmunk full of nuts.

"Kanye West," they said simultaneously. Makenzie laughed so hard that tears ran down her face. "What the heck you got in your mouth?"

"Cotton balls," Chris said as he pulled one out his mouth. They all laughed.

Chris climbed in the front seat next to Mya while Issayah hopped in the back. They headed east on 147th Street then merged on the I-94 Expressway. Traffic ran smoothly until they reached the downtown area where they ran into a traffic jam. It took them an hour and fifteen minutes to reach the amusement park.

They parked the vehicle then walked the long distance to the entrance. They paid, had the reentry mark stamped on their hands then walked into the graveyard themed scene. Makenzie grabbed Issayah's arm and pulled him close when she saw the tombstones, haunted mazes and costumed ghouls everywhere. This was her first time visiting Six Flags Great America on a Fright Fest night.

Makenzie loved scary movies so she thought this would be her cup of tea. She screamed when she saw a group of zombies heading towards them. She jumped behind Issayah, closed her eyes and buried her face in the center of his back.

"Makenzie, I know you're not scared. Not the #1 fan of any and all scary movies," Mya teased. "Here take my picture with this zombie," she said as she handed Chris her cell phone.

"Yeah, but that's on the screen. This is crazy. I'm going to be having nightmares," Makenzie said as she looked around the park.

"I got you boo. I wish one of these zombies would run up on my girl," Issayah said as he turned around to give Makenzie a kiss.

"Look. They're dancing off Michael Jackson's Thriller," Chris said walking towards the crowd.

Makenzie, Mya and Issayah followed him. What looked like thirty zombies, of all shapes and sizes, moved to the rhythm of the music as the crowd took pictures and danced along. Mya climbed on Chris' back to get a better view and Makenzie followed suit. The Michael Jackson wannabe lead the crew in his red leather jacket and flooding pants as smoke filled the air.

"Get it Mike," Issayah shouted.

After the Thriller show, they rode roller coasters, braved haunted houses and witnessed a resurrection. Rides soon began to shut down for the night as the park neared closing time. As they followed the crowd towards the exit, Makenzie and her friends laughed about her jumping on Issayah's back in the haunted house they'd just left.

"Oowee, I want a funnel cake before we leave!" Makenzie pulled Issayah towards a nearby cafe. They stood in line for fifteen minutes before arriving at the register.

"Can I have a funnel cake with extra strawberries and whip cream?" Makenzie asked as she pulled some money out her front pocket.

"Would you like something to drink?" The cashier asked right before she blew her nose in a Kleenex sitting next to the register.

"Umm, no." Makenzie turned towards Issayah and frowned, grossed out by her actions.

The cashier took Makenzie's money, gave her the change and headed towards the already made funnel cakes. She picked up a plate and proceeded to put strawberries on top.

"I know that's not my funnel cake you're making!" Makenzie snapped.

"Yeah, what's the problem? You said extra strawberries and cream right?"

"You just finished blowing your nasty nose. That's the problem. On top of that you didn't wash your hands or put any gloves on and now you think I'm going to eat that?" Makenzie rolled her eyes and twisted her neck as she spoke.

The other customers turned to see what all the commotion was about.

"I'm sorry. I didn't realize...

"How can you not realize that you blew your nose and then went to fix someone's food? You can give that to whoever you want but it won't be me. No telling how many people got boogers in their funnel cake today messing with you."

"No, that was the first time I blew my nose today," the cashier tried defending herself.

"Whatever," Makenzie said waving her off. "Excuse me. You in the glasses back there, can you make my funnel cake?"

"Umm, yeah sure," the tall, red haired boy in the blue shirt answered hesitantly.

"Your hands are clean right?"

"Yes and I have on gloves," he answered as he picked up a fresh funnel cake.

"Cool." She took one last look at the cashier and shook her head.

"You be cutting up. I'm gonna have to watch you. Why you embarrass that girl like that?" Issayah asked.

"She was bogus for that. That's just nasty. You'd rather let her fix your food and risk getting her germs than to speak out?"

"I ain't saying all that. I'm just saying you could've confronted her on the low."

"I could've but I bet she'll think twice before doing some nasty stuff like that again to someone else."

They headed out the door and met back up with Mya and Chris who were sitting on a bench nearby. They exited the park and headed towards the car.

"Awe, hell naw! If it ain't the psycho herself."

They all turned to see Makenzie's ex-boyfriend Jordan, his boy Devon and another guy looking directly at them. Makenzie's heart sped up faster than a Mustang GT on an open freeway. Her right palm instantly turned hot and sweaty right in Issayah's hand. She couldn't believe this was happening. Of all the people in the world, she had to run into Jordan.

"Man, this you?" Jordan said pointing to Makenzie.

"Yeh, who's asking?" Issayah looked Jordan up and down with a mean mug.

"Just call me smart because I left her alone," Jordan said sarcastically.

"Whatever, Jordan. Didn't you try to call me just last week?" Makenzie said with her hands on her hips. "I sent you straight to voicemail because I didn't have nothing to say to you then and I don't have nothing to say to you now."

"I called because i realized you still had my Bulls hat and I'm going to a game next week, not because I'm trying to get back with you. Believe that!"

"I tossed that out a long time ago with the rest of the trash that had me tied to you. As you can see I have a real man so forget you ever met me. Let's go ya'll," Makenzie said.

"It's cool. I brought a new one anyway. I'm glad you moved on and finally stopped stalking me. Let me ask your new man something though? Has she showed you her alter ego yet?" Jordan turned his attention towards Issayah.

Issayah looked puzzled. He wondered what this guy was talking about.

"Naw, probably not, but it won't be long before it attacks. It ain't nothing nice either. I suggest you run while you still have time. She's nuts dude," Jordan and his boys laughed.

Makenzie was hot inside. She couldn't believe Jordan was standing there fronting her off, trying to make her look like a fool in front of Issayah. If he didn't care about her anymore why was he making such a big scene? His mouth was running nonstop and she couldn't take it anymore.

Gloria Dotson-Lewis

"I'll show your punk butt psycho!" Makenzie said as she ran up on Jordan, lifted her funnel cake in the air and smashed it in his face sending him stumbling back. She balled her small hands into fists and started swinging on Jordan. He couldn't see with the whipped cream in his eyes so he placed his arms in front of his face to block the blows. People standing by laughed as they looked on in amazement.

Issayah grabbed Makenzie around the waist and pulled her off Jordan. She continued to curse him out as she tried to escape his grip.

"Makenzie, calm down." Mya tried to reason with her.

"Bump that! He's standing up here trying to clown me." Makenzie said as she smoothed her misplaced hair back into a ponytail.

"Let's just go. He's not even worth it," Mya said.

Jordan finally got the whipped cream out of his face and lunged towards Makenzie but Issayah stood in front of her with his arm extended protecting her from any harm.

"Man, I know you're embarrassed but you may as well get in your car and head home cause I'm not about to let you touch her," Issayah braced himself for a fight.

"I guarantee you don't want none of this man. What you better do is get her before she ends up in jail for violating her probation," Jordan shouted.

"You still talking Jordan! Let me go," Makenzie said as she struggled to free herself from Issayah.

"Calm down," Issayah said to Makenzie as he tightened his grip. "Look I ain't come out here to get into a fight but if you try to run up on her you gone get smashed today," Issayah said to Jordan.

It's cool, it's cool, she ain't worth it anyway. " Jordan said as he turned to walk away with his fist balled up by his sides.

You Got Me Twisted

Issayah relaxed his muscles and took a deep breath glad that the situation was over and done with. He didn't understand what had just happened. One minute he was having a good time and the next minute some guy he'd never seen before started saying all these crazy things about his girl. He didn't know what to think.

Jordan didn't move ten feet before he turned back around and rushed Issayah, sucker punching him in the left eye. Issayah quickly composed himself and swung back, hitting him in the stomach several times, knocking the wind out of him as he fell back to the ground. Jordan's boys moved in to help their friend. Chris tossed his cell phone to Mya ready to ride with his boy.

"Security is coming," A male voice shouted from the crowd just as the gang fight began.

Chris briskly pulled Issayah off Jordan and told the girls to follow them as they headed towards the car. Jordan's boys helped him off the ground and walked in the opposite direction. They were all gone just as security pulled up.

When they reached the vehicle, they returned to their original seats. Mya slowly pulled out of the parking space, careful to avoid hitting any of the many pedestrians walking through the lot. Traffic moved at a snail's pace as hundreds of cars navigated through five exit gates.

"Are you okay? Your eye is swollen," Makenzie said as she held Issayah's chin in her hand.

"What the hell was that all about? Who was ole' boy?" Issayah moved his head.

"Just this guy I use to date."

"A nobody," Mya chimed in.

"Well dude is lucky security came when they did because he was about to get a serious beat down," Chris said as he punched the palm of his hand.

Gloria Dotson-Lewis

"You're on probation?" Issayah looked at Makenzie with squinted eyes.

"Jordan is just mad because I left him alone," Makenzie lied, avoiding the question. "He's a punk. I don't know what I ever saw in him."

"Yeah, he's definitely a punk. He sucker punched my boy and still got his butt whooped. Little Mayweather back there ain't nothing to mess with," Chris said as he held his fist over his shoulder for a pound.

"Naw, that's Ms. Mayweather back there. I still can't believe you smashed that funnel cake in his face," Mya said. They all laughed.

"I guess I better not get on your bad side," Issayah said.

"Haha, I see ya'll got jokes."

chapter 10

It was unusually warm for a November morning in Chicago and the surrounding suburbs. The sun was shining and there was no snow in the forecast for the day. It was Thanksgiving morning and Makenzie and her mother were up finishing the meal they had begun cooking last night. Although Rhonda had to work today, she wanted to come home to her traditional Thanksgiving Day feast.

Makenzie found pleasure in cooking and this was the one time she actually enjoyed spending with her mother. When she was younger her mother and father would cook meals together and she would be right there helping out. She even had her own apron with the words 'little helper' on the front. While her father did most of the cooking her mother whipped up the desserts. Those were the moments she cherished as a family.

Back then, most of the family gatherings took place at their home unless they went out of town to spend the holiday with Rhonda's family in Cincinnati, Ohio which was usually every other year. Now the gatherings were held at her fraternal grandmother's house on the south side in the city.

"Makenzie, check on the sweet potato pies for me please," Rhonda said as she prepared a small peach cobbler to go into the oven next.

"I think they have about ten more minutes and then they should be good," Makenzie said as she closed the oven door.

"I'm glad we got all the main course dishes out of the way last night. We'll be all finished once the cobbler and pound cake are done. I wish I could spend the day with you but if I don't work, we don't eat."

"Everything smells so good. I can't wait to eat but I have to save some room for Grandma P's cooking. I'm looking forward to seeing her and all the family. We always have a good time playing games and having dance contests."

"Yeah, make sure you tell everyone I said hello. Your dad usually works on the holidays too. So, you may not get to see him unless you get over there before he leaves for work."

"I hope Grandma P cooked her corn casserole this year. That stuff is the bomb. I'll have to ask her for the recipe so I can try to make it next year," Makenzie said quickly changing the subject.

She did not want to be bothered with her father and was glad he had to work. He was required to rotate weekends and holidays with his co-workers at the hospital and this year was his turn to work on Thanksgiving. There was no way she was going to arrive early to run into him.

When Walter left Makenzie and her mom, he would come around smelling like one of the winos outside of the liquor store near her grandmother's house. He started drinking while he was still residing with them but the drinking got a lot worse once he moved out. Makenzie would sometimes hear her mother fussing at him about coming over drunk and make him leave. Then, there were other times he appeared to be sober but still smelled like a bottle of Vodka. She was forced to spend time with him during those times but when she got older and started participating in sports and extracurricular activities, she began using them as excuses to avoid having to see him so much. It wasn't long after that when their relationship grew farther and farther apart.

You Got Me Twisted

After all the desserts where out of the oven, Rhonda went to shower and dress for work. Makenzie was watching television in the family room when her mother came down the stairs in her navy blue pants and light blue long sleeve polo shirt with the CTA logo on the sleeve. She was a Bus Operator for the Chicago Transit Authority and worked all kinds of crazy hours. She picked up her keys and stepped in the family room.

"I'm about to leave. Your Aunt Jamela will be here around 2 p.m. to pick you up," she said as she leaned down to kiss Makenzie's cheek. "Have a nice Thanksgiving. I love you."

"Yeah, she texted me," Makenzie said as she gave her mother a quick hug then turned her attention back to the television.

After Rhonda left for work, Makenzie fixed her a small plate of deep fried turkey, macaroni and cheese, collard greens and dressing. She watched a couple of reruns of *Everybody Hates Chris* and then took a nap. She had four more hours before her aunt would be there to pick her up. When her alarm went off at 1pm, she hit the snooze button twice before finally getting out the bed and in the shower.

"Hello," Makenzie said into her cellular phone as she rubbed lotion on her legs.

"What's up cuz? Are you ready because we're about to scoop you up?" Her cousin Malkomb asked.

"By the time you guys get here I'll be ready. I wait to see you cuz. It seems like forever."

He was her aunt Jamela's only son. They were really close growing up but they hadn't seen each other in over a year. Malkomb hadn't long gotten out of jail on a drug charge. He stayed in and out of trouble with the law. It started when he was only thirteen, stealing candy at the

Gloria Dotson-Lewis

neighborhood store then it graduated to stealing cars and selling drugs.

When Jamela and his father, Malkomb Sr., divorced things really got out of hand. He and his mother moved back to Grandma P's house and his father moved two hours away. Malkomb Sr. started seeing another woman and Malkomb starting seeing less of his father. He would promise to take Malkomb to the movies or to a baseball game then never show up. It wasn't long before he began getting into fights at school and hanging with the wrong crowd in the neighborhood.

"I can't wait to kick your butt on the Kinect. I'm killing the Michael Jackson Experience now."

"Never that. I come in first place every year and this year won't be no different."

"You wanna make a bet? I'll bet you a chicken sandwich from Chick-fil-A," Makenzie challenged.

"Add a shake and you got a bet," Malkomb added.

"It's on! I've been practicing over Mya's house with her little brother so I got all those moves down."

"I ain't seen Mya in a minute. How is her fine butt doing anyway? I thought you was gone hook us up?"

"Nope, I never said that. Don't even try it. Do you remember how you played my girl Casey when I introduced you to her a couple of years ago? You dogged her out."

"Casey, what are you doing here? I told you to call before you come over," Malkomb said when he opened his front door.

"I've been calling you since last night. I left you at least ten messages. Didn't you get em?" Casey asked as she looked at him with red puffy eyes.

"I ain't had time to check my messages but that's not the

point. I keep telling you I don't like nobody popping up unannounced."

"I'm not just anybody Malkomb. I'm your girl and I should be able to pop up anytime, answer your phone and whatever else unless you got something to hide. And, why are we standing in the doorway?"

"The only way you gone check my phone is if you're paying that $100 bill every month. And you're not coming in because you can't follow directions, phone first."

"Why are you tripping? Is this how you treat somebody you claim you love?

"Look, I'm just gone be real wit you Casey. You're cool but I don't think we gone work out," Malkomb said coldly

"What? Are you joking because if you are it's not funny? You said you loved me." A tear ran down her face as she gently brushed her hand over Malkomb's left cheek.

"You're cool but I just need some space. Things are moving too fast for me. I ain't ready to be on lock down," he said, removing her hand from his face.

"Please don't do this to me. I love you Malkomb. I let you be my first. Don't that mean anything to you?"

Malkomb didn't respond. He looked past her at a girl walking her dog down his block. He tried to break it off nicely with Casey a couple times but she didn't get the hint so this time he was taking a stronger approach.

"We can slow things down. Just tell me what you want me to do," Casey pleaded through the tears now racing down her face like Niagara Falls.

"There's nothing you can do shorty, but let me give you a little advice. Guys don't like females to sweat them. It's a turn off. You need to fall back some," Malkomb said then closed the door in Casey's face.

"What? I didn't dog that girl out. She was a pest. I should be mad at you for hooking me up to that stalker. She used to call my phone like fifty times a day and if I didn't answer she'd pop up at the crib. I had to curse her out to get her up off me."

"How did you think she was gonna act? You were her first. That girl was in love with you. She used to get on my nerves 'Malkombing' me to death," Makenzie said.

"I do have that effect on the ladies."

"Yeah, whatever."

"Malkomb, let's go boy." Makenzie could hear her aunt yelling.

"Aight cuz, we'll be there in a minute so be ready."

Makenzie threw on her blue jean Gap skirt, winter white sweater and matching UGG boots then combed her thick hair into a ponytail. Once dressed she lied across her bed and bobbed her head and rocked her feet to the music stored in her Ipod. She left one ear unplugged so she could listen out for the car horn or cell phone.

When they arrived she grabbed her coat, turned on the porch light and locked the door. Malkomb was sitting in the driver's seat of his mother's black four door Jeep Cherokee while Aunt Jamela sat securely fastened on the passenger's side. Makenzie hopped in the back seat, leaned forward and gave them both a hug.

"When did he get his license? Are you sure we're safe Aunt Jamela?" Makenzie cracked.

"I know how to drive. My dad taught me how to drive when I was twelve. He started out taking me in empty parking lots and then on the streets. I'm just legal now."

"I could've choked your father when I found out he was letting you drive his car while you were visiting him. I couldn't figure out why you drove so well when I took you for your driving exam. I called all my friends bragging about how you didn't appear to be nervous and you followed all the rules of the road. Then, come to find out you'd been driving for a couple of years already," Aunt Jamela said while shaking her head side to side.

"And now I'm your personal chauffeur and errand boy," Malkomb joked.

"That's right. You want to use my car when you go out with your friends then it's going to cost you."

Aunt Jamela turned around and held her palm in the air for Makenzie to give her high-five. They laughed and talked about old times as they drove the thirty minute distance to Grandma P's house. When they pulled on the block, parked cars filled the streets. They had to pull in a spot on the next block and walk back to the house.

Grandma P opened the door and Makenzie fell right into her arms. She gently squeezed her full waist then kissed her cheek. She loved her grandmother but didn't get to see her as often as she used to. Once her father moved back to Grandma P's house Makenzie stopped going over to visit unless she needed some money from her father or it was a holiday gathering taking place.

Grandma P was her caregiver from birth until the age of five when she began kindergarten then she kept her afterschool until she began junior high. Makenzie stayed with her until her mother or father picked her up after they got off of work. They would go to the grocery stores, shopping malls and her friend Emma's house to watch soap operas. Most of her summer was spent at Grandma P's house too, along with Malkomb, her half brother Kalvin and her cousin Trish. They were all just a few years apart and inseparable. The adults in the family called them the four musketeers.

Kalvin's mother relocated to Michigan taking him with her when he was only ten. He returned to Chicago every year for two months in the summer and a few other times throughout the year. Trish's parents, Uncle George and Aunt Yolanda, moved her to Atlanta when she was nine. She always came for a couple of weeks during the summer which was the only time they all got a chance to be together at the same time.

When Kalvin and Trish moved Makenzie and Malkomb became closer. Whenever Makenzie's parents would take her on family outings to the Museum of Science and Industry, Navy Pier or Shedd Aquarium, Malkomb was right there with them. Whenever Makenzie had news to share, good or bad, Malkomb was the first person she called. When he went to jail she felt deserted. They were not only cousins but best friends.

"Ohhh, how is my baby? I've missed you so much," Grandma P said as she hugged Makenzie around the neck.

"I missed you too. I've been so busy with school but I'll try to get by here more often," Makenzie quickly lied. The only way she would come around more is if her dad moved out and got his own place.

"My pretty little Kenzi Pooh is growing up so fast," Grandma P pinched Makenzie's cheeks. "You look just like your daddy."

Makenzie cringed. She hated when people said that. Everyone who saw her dad said the same thing. She looked down so her grandmother couldn't see the look of disgust on her face.

"I'm starving. Can I get something to eat?" She needed to get the image of her father out of her head and quick.

"Go hang your coat in the hall closet and fix yourself

something to eat child."

Makenzie walked past the living room and down the narrow hall to the closet. The air was filled with food, cigarette smoke, music and conversation. She stopped to embrace and talk to loved ones she hadn't seen in a while before reaching the dining room where all the food was set up. All the entrees were on one table, vegetables and other side dishes were placed on another and desserts covered another. Malkomb pushed Makenzie aside and grabbed a Styrofoam plate and plastic utensils.

"Boy, how you gone jump in front of me? Makenzie slapped Malkomb on the back. Don't you have any respect for ladies?"

"What lady? All I see is you standing here."

"That was stale Dusty."

"Dusty? Man ain't nobody called me that in years. Kill that."

"I've been calling you that since we were little."

"Little is the key word. I'll be eighteen in three months. I'm not a kid anymore. Besides, who wants to be called Dusty of all names? Who started that mess in the first place?" Malkomb asked as he stacked his plate with food.

"Grandma P started that because you loved to play in the dirt when we were little, hahaha."

"Well, do this fine face look like it plays in dirt anymore? " Malkomb brushed his left hand over his hairless chin.

"Please. Just because these rats be chasing after you don't mean you're fine. Rats like everything. Besides, you'll always be little Dusty to me," Makenzie chuckled.

"When I get with your girl Mya, she'll let you know that there ain't nothing little about me."

"You so nasty. And you and Mya ain't gone happen so get over it."

"All I'm gone say is don't be surprised if we pull up in front of your crib together one day."

"Whateva." Makenzie rolled her eyes at her cousin then went to find a seat in the crowded house.

After eating, they went to the basement. It was a large, brightly lit open room. The furniture was repositioned to accommodate all the relatives occupying its space. It was obvious that this area was designated for the children and younger adults. You had Guesstures going on in one corner, Taboo in another and Chutes and Ladders in yet another. Then there was a group playing games on the Xbox Kinect console game system.

Makenzie was ready to kick Malkomb's butt but a couple of their younger relatives were already playing basketball.

They found a spot in the corner of the room to chill. When their turn finally came around, Malkomb hit the eject button and replaced the disk then grabbed a remote. Makenzie followed his lead and stood in front of the sixty-five inch television set.

They danced along with Michael and his crew while everyone in the room cheered them on. The excitement escalated when they got to the final dance off. Each had won one round. This last game would determine who would have bragging rights until next time. They moved their bodies to the rhythm of the music like their lives depended on it. The score was close as the song neared its end. When the game stopped, all the girls in the room jumped up and down cheering. Makenzie had beat Malkomb two out of three games and was now this year's champion.

"In your face!" Makenzie shouted in Malkomb's direction.

"It's cool. I let you win anyway."

"Don't be a sore loser!" What I need to know is what day

you're taking me to get my chicken sandwich and milkshake?" Makenzie asked, with a huge smile spread across her face.

"How about never?"

"If you play me like that . . . "

While Makenzie and Malkomb argued back and forth, her aunt Jamela came down stairs and told everyone to come up. She stated Grandma P had a surprise for everyone. The kids started pushing each other aside to get up the stairs first.

"I wonder what Grandma P is up to," Makenzie said.

"I don't have a clue," Malkomb said with a smirk on his face.

"Why are you looking like that? You know something don't you?" Makenzie pulled him around by the arm to face her.

"I might but you'll just have to wait and see," Malkomb said as he headed up the stairs two at a time with a huge smile on his face.

"I thought I was your favorite cousin. How are you gone keep secrets from me," she said following closely after him.

"Everyone here?" Grandma P asked.

"Yes momma, go ahead with the surprise," Jamela excitedly responded.

"Ok. First I'd like to say that I'm so happy that the Lord has blessed me with another opportunity to have all my loved ones here with me today. I love each and every one of you with all my heart. But, today is very special to me," Grandma P paused as tears ran down her cheeks.

Makenzie elbowed Malkomb. "What the heck is going on?"

"Just wait and see. You are going to flip out."

"Come on in baby," Grandma P waived towards someone standing on the back porch.

Gloria Dotson-Lewis

Makenzie's eyes stretched as wide as a saucer. Her heart began to race as her body trembled. She wanted to run out the front door and never look back but her feet felt like they were stuck in cement. Everyone seemed so happy about Grandma P's surprise, clapping and cheering. But, Makenzie suddenly felt like vomiting.

"I know it's been a long time but I know you know who that is right?" Malkomb asked Makenzie.

She tried to speak but no words would come out. Tears started pouring from her eyes.

"I knew you'd be happy but I didn't think you would cry. Go give your brother a hug girl."

Makenzie felt a warm liquid run down her leg and realized she had urinated on herself. She ran to the upstairs bathroom and locked the door. She sat on the edge of the tub and balled her eyes out. She wanted to go home right now. If she wasn't so high up, she'd escape through the window.

"Makenzie, what is wrong with you girl? You haven't seen Kalvin in about four years. I thought you'd be happy to see him. Are you mad because he didn't keep in touch or something?" Malkomb leaned his ear against the door to listen for a response.

"I don't feel so good. Can you please drive me home?"

"Yeah, open the door."

"I need you to go in Grandma P's drawer and get me a pair of her jogging pants with the draw string in them."

"What? Why?" Malkomb scratched the side of his head.

"Just do it please," Makenzie shouted.

"Ok, chill," he said, shaking his head.

Makenzie got a face towel out the small linen closet next to the tub and washed her lower body in the sink. When Malkomb tapped on the door, she cracked it open and pulled the pants through the small opening. She changed, rolled her wet pants up like a scroll, walked out the bathroom then straight out the door, ignoring everyone who tried to stop her.

She walked swiftly down the street as Malkomb tried to catch up. She wanted nothing more than to get in her bed and pull the comforter over her head. Malkomb pressed the remote to unlock the doors. He started the engine and pulled out into traffic.

"Now that we're alone, can you tell me what the hell is going on?"

"Only if you promise not to tell a soul."

chapter 11

Makenzie hadn't eaten much or gotten much sleep in the last two days. It was now three a.m. and she was tired of tossing and turning so she turned on her night light and flipped to page thirty-nine in her book *Snitch*, by J.L. Wilson. Flashbacks of Thanksgiving kept creeping in her mind and she needed to get lost in the pages to elude those thoughts.

Makenzie hadn't talked to Issayah since the morning of Thanksgiving. She knew they would both be busy with family for the holiday but expected to talk to him that following day. She was upset and hurt when he didn't call her. She needed to talk to him. He always made her feel better. She called him but didn't get an answer. She figured he would see her missed call on the caller I.D. so she opted not to leave a message.

After hours had passed and no word from Issayah, her mind started to fill with all kinds of scenarios of why he hadn't called yet. One moment she pictured him with some other female, the next moment she pictured him on the side of the road in an accident then back to him and some girl hanging out. She had several different emotions going on at one time; heartache, anger and worry. Makenzie's anger eventually won the war in her head so she decided to text him.

What r u doing that u cant call me back? I know u c I called u! U must b with some other chick. U know what, 4get it, dont call me ever again. I don't have time for the games.

You Got Me Twisted

She pressed the send button on her touch screen phone then called her girl Mya.

"Hey chick, what's up? How was your turkey day?" Mya started talking as soon as she picked up the phone.

"It was cool," Makenzie said telling a half truth. She wasn't calling to discuss Thanksgiving. She needed to vent about Issayah.

"Girl, why haven't I heard from Issayah all day today? He calls me every day. I tried calling him several times but he's not picking up. So, I just sent him a text message dumping his butt."

"What? He could have a perfectly legit reason why he's not calling you back Makenzie. You could at least hear him out before you kick him to the curb."

"Yesterday was our three month anniversary and he didn't even call me. Forget him. He's probably with some rat," Makenzie said before smacking her lips.

"I doubt it! I think you're being overly dramatic. Issayah is the sweetest guy you've ever dated and he's so into you. I just think you need to relax and give him a chance to explain."

"I'm not the one to let guys run game on me. I don't have time for a million excuses. If you do right, there's no need to explain anything. Remember when your ex-boyfriend Jewon used to lie to you about being at football practice all the time until you finally busted him at the show? You should've been through with him that day. He told you it was a group of them and he wasn't with a female but you saw him hugging that girl with your own eyes. Then you turned around and forgave him. Could not have been me."

"You right. I was stupid for that but love makes you do some crazy things. You know about that first hand. I still laugh at how you jacked up Jordan's car when you thought

73

he was cheating on you."

"I still say he should've told me he was hanging out with his cousin. Sometimes people bring things on themselves. Had he picked up the phone and told me what was up, the situation would never have happened," Makenzie said hutching her shoulders.

"I guess you're right but it was still funny."

After ending her call with Mya, Makenzie finally fell back to sleep. She was awakened by a chirping bird outside her window. She was glad it was Saturday and she didn't have to go to school. When she looked at the clock on her desk, she realized she only slept three additional hours. She laid back down and stared at the ceiling, remembering the pain she felt before she drifted off to sleep.

Makenzie wiped the cold out of her eyes then slowly forced herself out of bed. She made her way down the hall, past her mother's room to the bathroom. The small, peach colored space was filled with the scent of vanilla potpourri. She washed her face, brushed her teeth then rinsed her mouth with Listerine.

As she headed back to her room she peeked in her mother's bedroom door. When she saw the empty, neatly made bed, she recalled that her mother had to be at work early that morning so she pulled the door shut. As she crossed the entryway to her room she noticed a note, folded in half resting on the keyboard of her computer.

I have to work overtime and won't be home until 8p.m. Make sure you clean this junkie room of yours. I love you and I'll call to check on you later.
Mom

Makenzie rolled her eyes, balled the paper up and tossed

it in the trash can next to her desk. She flopped back on her bed and searched for the cell phone hiding in her blanket. She pushed the green button to see if she had any missed calls.

"Oh now he calls after I dump his butt. Well, he's going to have to wait and worry like he made me do."

She pressed the voicemail button to listen to the message Issayah left for her.

Makenzie, what's up with the text you left me? I told you I had drama practice all day yesterday. Call me when you get this message.

Makenzie made her bed, straightened up her cluttered dresser and Swiffer dusted her hardwood floor. Afterward, she went down stairs, fixed herself a bowl of Fruity Pebbles and ate in front of the television. Issayah called two more times but Makenzie sent his calls straight to voicemail. As she sat with her legs crossed Chinese style in an oversized, red lounge chair, she was startled by the door bell.

It must be the UPS man delivering those boots I ordered the other day.

She peered through the rectangular shaped window in the center of the oak wood door. She saw a white, blue and orange Bears skull cap and knew right away that it was Issayah. She unlocked the deadbolt and cracked the door.

"What are you doing here? Didn't you get my message? We are over."

"You didn't listen to the voice messages I left you? I told you I was in drama practice all day yesterday. I didn't get home until eleven and I was dead tired. I got in the shower and went to bed in ten minutes," Issayah said as visible breath from the cold air exited his mouth.

Gloria Dotson-Lewis

"What if I say I don't believe you? You could've texted me to let me know you was tired and would call me the next day. How simple is that? "

"You're right baby. I'm sorry. Had I known you were going to ax me over it, I would have called . . . better yet I would've come by. Can a brother come in? It's cold out here."

"Who says I can have company?" Makenzie said as she pulled the door open a little wider.

"Your mother's car is gone so I know you're here alone. Quit playing and let me in girl," Issayah said when he saw a slight smile on Makenzie's face.

"I guess I'll let you slide this once but I'm not that chick that gives a million chances so get your stuff together," Makenzie said as she locked the door, then switched past Issayah.

He grabbed her from behind and kissed her on the neck. Makenzie closed her eyes as she felt that tingling sensation shoot through her body. His touch did something to her she couldn't understand. She turned around, stood on her tip toes and placed both arms around his neck. She kissed him softly on the lips and Issayah responded back with his tongue.

"Let's go up to your room," Issayah said as he continued kissing her.

"Okay."

She grabbed his hand and led him up the stairs and to the left. She was now glad she had cleaned her room like her mother told her. Issayah sat on the foot of her bed and pulled Makenzie between his legs. He pulled her shirt up and kissed her flat, unblemished stomach. Makenzie felt the tingling travel through her body again but this time is was more intense. She threw her head back and allowed him to explore her body.

You Got Me Twisted

Issayah's cellular phone vibrated twice and then rang. He and Makenzie continued making out ignoring the annoying interruption. When it rang two more times Makenzie stepped out of Issayah's embrace and rolled her eyes.

"Who keeps blowing up your phone like that?"

"Probably one of my boys. Who cares? Come here," Issayah said as he pulled his phone out of his front pocket and tossed it to the side.

The phone rang again. Makenzie looked at Issayah as he picked it up and checked the caller i.d. His eyebrows dropped as he looked at the number in confusion. Makenzie became suspicious and grabbed the phone out of Issayah's hand and stepped back out of his arms. The name Robyn was displayed on the screen.

"Robyn! Why is Robyn blowing up your phone like that?" She threw the phone, faster than lightening, hitting him in the forehead.

"Girl, what you do that for?" He leaned forward and grabbed his head.

"Don't act all innocent. Why is a she calling your phone?" Makenzie screamed while slapping him in the head.

Issayah grabbed Makenzie's wrists and shook her. "Makenzie, cool out! What is wrong with you girl?

"Let me go!" Makenzie struggled to free her hands.

"Are you going to calm down so I can let you go and explain?"

"You better explain."

Issayah slowly loosened his grip. Makenzie slapped him one last time then waited for him to start talking.

Issayah shook it off. "Makenzie chill! It's probably about the play we got coming up."

"That girl likes you. She is not worried about no darn play."

Gloria Dotson-Lewis

"What? Robyn and I are just cool. It's not even like that."

"Yeah right! You need to call her back right now so we can see what she's calling you for. It's Saturday so I know ya'll don't have practice. You must think I have stupid written across my forehead or something," she said as she pushed him in the head with her index finger to try to get him to look up at her.

"You need to go get me some ice for this knot," Issayah said as he pointed to his face.

"Issayah, you better call her now or you'll have more than a knot."

Makenzie leaned to one side and placed her hands on her hips. Issayah shook his head and slowly picked up his phone.

"Man, this is crazy. You better be glad I like you. I want an apology when you see it ain't about nothing," he said as he pressed the redial button and put the phone up to his ear.

"Oh hell naw, put it on speaker so I can hear," Makenzie demanded.

The phone rang twice before Robyn picked up. "What's up Issayah? Why didn't you answer when I called the first time?"

"I was busy. What's up?"

"Deg, it's like that? I thought we were better than that."

Makenzie's left eyebrow went up and her nose flared like a bull. She stood silent to hear what Issayah would say next.

"I'm over my girl's house. Did you need something?"

"I was calling to see if you wanted to get together today to practice our lines."

"Naw boo boo, it's Saturday and he'll be hanging out with me today so you need to find someone else to practice with," Makenzie jumped in.

"Who is that? Do you have me on speaker?" Robyn

asked.

"You have a problem with that? 'Cause I know you don't have nothing private to talk to my man about."

"Is that Makenzie? Booboo you don't have to feel insecure. Issayah and I are just friends. I have to communicate with him because of the play so you may as well relax."

"I don't have anything to be insecure about sweetie so you can gone with all that. You have no reason to call his phone when you see him all week long. Sounds like you need to get a life if all you have to think about is practicing lines on the weekend."

"Are you his bodyguard or girlfriend? Can he speak for himself? Because us practicing on weekends have never been a problem before."

"Trick, I'm tired of your mouth--"

"Robyn, I'll holla at you on Monday, ok?" Issayah intervened before it got any uglier. They were now screaming at each other. He quickly disconnected the call.

"What did she mean by it's never been a problem before Issayah? You've never told me anything about practicing with Robyn on weekends."

"Because, I don't be practicing with Robyn. I mean, yeah, she be there with us practicing but it's not just me and her like you're thinking."

"Get it together cause it sounds like a bunch of BS to me."

"You can ask my boy, Alex. He'll tell you that it's always a group of us when we get together."

"Well, ole girl likes you. You better tell her not to call you anymore. She can see you in school," Makenzie spoke as she twisted her neck and was flinging her hands.

"I can't believe you tripping like this. It's not even like

that with Robyn."

"Yeah right. Whatever Issayah. Check your girl before I check her."

chapter 1a

"ow are you Makenzie?" Dr. Reid asked after taking a sip from her bottled water.

"Fine."

"We didn't get to meet last week because of the holiday. Speaking of, how was your Thanksgiving?"

"It was cool," Makenzie said diverting her eyes to the floor.

"Did you spend it with your mom?"

"No, she had to work. I went over my grandmother's house."

"Did you enjoy yourself?"

"It had been a while since I last saw her and some of the other family so it was cool," Makenzie looked back up with a smile in her eyes.

"Is there a reason you don't get to see your grandmother much?"

"My dad's been living with her ever since he left me and my mom. I don't want to deal with him so I just don't go by there."

"How long ago did he leave?"

Makenzie's whole demeanor suddenly changed. She slouched back on the couch, and rolled her eyes. She didn't want to get into a deep discussion about her family. Most days she wished she could upgrade them for better parents. She hated them both but especially her father.

"Makenzie?" Can you tell me about your dad?" Dr. Reid

softly asked while tilting her head to the side interrupting Makenzie's thoughts.

"He left over three years ago. I was like twelve or thirteen I think. He became a drunk and I don't want to have anything to do with him. When he comes around he stinks and he's always apologizing. It gets on my nerves," Makenzie rolled her eyes again.

"That's a long time. Did it hurt you when he left?" Dr. Reid spoke softly.

"Yeah, but I got over it."

"Was he at home during Thanksgiving?"

"No, thank goodness. He had to work."

"Why are you mad at your father? Is it because he left you and your mom?"

"That's part of it."

"Were you two very close?"

Makenzie's eyes instantly became glassy. She had never talked to anyone about her relationship with her father. But, her sessions with Dr. Reid hadn't been so bad lately. She was cool and down to earth not like that counselor her mother had her seeing when she was younger. She seemed to really care about what Makenzie had to say. She no longer felt like Dr. Reid was just trying to get all up in her business. But, the topic was still pretty touchy.

She nervously picked at her nails and nodded her head up and down. She quickly caught a tear before it raced down her face.

"Tell me about the dad you were close to."

Makenzie closed her eyes and spoke. "We were super close. If he was in the garage fixing on his car, I was right there handing him the tools. I even watched sports with him all the time. My mom said I used to wait outside the bathroom until he came out when I was only two,"

Makenzie chuckled at the memory.

Dr. Reid remained silent only smiling and nodding her head to show she was giving her full attention.

"He taught me how to read before I went to school. He taught me how to cook, ride a bike, swim, play the piano, everything. There wasn't anything he wouldn't do for me," Makenzie said, then took a deep breath.

"Do you know why he left?"

Makenzie turned her head and closed her eyes. Memories of that terrible day flooded her mind like a Tsunami. Her heart rate sped up and her voice shook as words tried to force their way out.

"Can we talk about something else?" Makenzie asked.

"Okay, maybe we can discuss that another day."

"Maybe."

"Can we talk about the incident with Jordan? You spray painted his car. What made you so upset that day?"

Makenzie rolled her eyes. She did not want to talk about Jordan's punk butt either. She was so over him.

"It's really not worth talking about. It was his fault just as much as mine. He was trying to play all innocent that day in court."

"How so?"

"I had been calling Jordan that day and I didn't get an answer. So, I drove around to his crib. His car wasn't out front where he always parked so I pulled off. As I'm riding down 87th and King Drive I spot him going the other way with some chick in the car," Makenzie felt herself getting mad all over again.

"Sounds like you were upset."

"I was more than upset. I'm like, how he riding around with some other girl and I was just with him the day before. He was telling me he loved me, calling me his wifey."

Gloria Dotson-Lewis

"Did you go back to his house to confront him?"

"I drove back over there but he wasn't there. I called him again but he still didn't answer. So, I waited for about thirty minutes but no Jordan. I went home for a while then I went back over there around 11pm. His car was out there this time. I wanted to ring the bell but I knew his mother was home. I don't know why but the can of spray paint I had in my trunk came to mind. I use it to cover rust spots on my car until I can afford to get it done professionally. I opened my trunk, got it out and spray painted 'busted' on the hood of his car."

"Looking back, now that you know it was his cousin in the car, do you think he deserved having his car spray painted?" Dr. Reid asked.

"I think the whole thing could have been avoided had he answered his phone or told me the day before that he would be hanging out with his cousin. I mean yeah, I could've rode off but I was heated at the time. I apologized to him after court that day but at the end of the day, he can't say it was all my fault. Besides, Jordan had a track record for getting caught up. That time may have been his cousin but I busted him with other chicks before," Makenzie said as she rolled her neck.

"You also have a misdemeanor battery charge on your record as well. What happened then?" Dr. Reid read from a folder on her lap.

"That was not my fault either. That was a bogus charge," Makenzie's voice elevated.

"It sounds like when people upset you, you have a hard time expressing yourself through words and sometimes you resort to physical altercations."

"Maybe," Makenzie twisted her lips and hunched her shoulders nonchalantly.

You Got Me Twisted

"I think you would benefit from some anger management techniques. There are things you can do to keep your feelings in check because if you don't, I'm afraid you may end up hurting someone or being hurt yourself. This session is over but we'll pick it up here next week ok?"

Makenzie got out of her seat, stretched her torso and headed towards the door. She was a little irritated that Dr. Ried was bringing up all this old stuff so she didn't bother to say goodbye.

chapter 13

Makenzie helped Issayah several times with his lines for the play but she had never seen him perform before tonight. She had no clue that he was so talented. He played Oscar, the leading man who lost his wife in the suicide attacks at World Trade Center in New York on 9/11/01. She watched along with the audience, in awe, as he effortlessly recited his lines and moved about the stage so confidently. His body language and facial expressions were extremely convincing and pulled at all her emotional strings. There wasn't a dry eye in the auditorium.

When the play was over they received a standing ovation. The main cast members returned to the stage for their final introduction. Everyone clapped as each actor was announced but when Issayah's name was called, the crowd went wild.

"That's my baby right there!" Makenzie shouted.

"You crazy," Mya laughed. "You did not tell me Issayah was so good. You better hold on to him. He may be the next Idris Elba. I can't believe he has me sitting up here crying." Mya dabbed her eyes with the sleeve of her shirt.

"Idris is cool but my baby is more on a Will Smith level," Makenzie said as she pulled a pack of Kleenex from her oversized purse.

"Yeah, Will does have more skills, but I love me some Idris."

"I know. You have him all over your bedroom walls."

"And you know it! Your girl Robyn didn't do so bad either," Maya said, looking out the corner of her eye to see

You Got Me Twisted

Makenzie's reaction.

"She was okay, I guess. I'm glad she played the wife who got killed," Makenzie joked. "Her part was really too short to see if she had any real skills like my baby though."

"Yeah, she didn't have but a few lines. She didn't need a lot of practice for that."

"That's what I know. She just trying to be all up in Issayah's face calling him on weekends to practice lines. She gone keep messing around and get whooped."

They sat around talking as the auditorium slowly cleared out. The spacious assembly hall was newly remodeled after last year's fire. The freshly painted beige walls were accented with white columns. A new computer controlled roof mounted lighting system supplied better light for stage productions and the old rickety seats where replaced by sturdy new ones.

"Where is James? I'm surprised he didn't come to see his boy."

"They have a basketball game at Thornfeld tonight. He is over there getting the story so he can write up the sports section by the end of the week, remember?" Mya said.

"Oh yeah, that's right. I'm just about finished with my article on the rising obesity rate in American schools. I was shocked at some of the information that I found."

"I know one thing, if they start replacing my Flammin' Hot Cheese Doodles with fruit snacks, I'm going to have one less friend up in this school."

"I ain't trying to give up my Pepsi or Snickers either but girl I can see why Michelle Obama got involved with the obesity campaign. It's out of control. So many people are dying every year from it. It's not only about being overweight, some of these kids develop heart problems and depression. Who wants to deal with all that when you're so young?"

"It must have really touched you because you're starting to sound like you're going to start your own campaign," Mya joked.

"Whatever."

Issayah, Robyn and some of the other cast members appeared from back stage. They were now in their regular street clothes. Makenzie didn't like the way Robyn was resting her hand on Issayah's shoulder as they walked in her direction.

"Do you see this trick? Why is she touching my man?"

Makenzie got out her seat and walked in their direction. When Robyn noticed her coming, she dropped her arm and balled her fists tight. Issayah didn't like the look on Makenzie's face. He knew if he didn't do something quick something was going to go down. He increased his stride, grabbed Makenzie around the waist, lifted her in the air and kissed her on the lips.

"Hey baby. How did you like the show?"

"It was the bomb! You did so good baby. You had me and Mya crying like babies," Makenzie said, no longer concerned with Robyn.

"For real? That's what's up. Well, now it's time to celebrate. We're heading over to Beggar's Pizza. You coming?"

"Of course," Makenzie said. She knew she should've been heading home. Her mother told her to be home by eight. Ms. Pierce had to work overtime again and always called to check on Makenzie when she went on break. But there was no way she was going to give Robyn the opportunity to get closer to Issayah. He was so naïve. He didn't even realize that the girl was feeling him but Makenzie knew better.

You Got Me Twisted

"You coming Mya? Chris is going to meet us over there," Issayah smiled.

"Ain't nobody worrying about no Chris. I'm going because I'm hungry."

"Okay, if you say so," Issayah laughed.

"Makenzie get your boy."

They headed out of the auditorium towards the rear parking lot. Three cars loaded up and trailed down the street to their destination. After a thirty minute wait, the host guided them to an area were two tables were pushed together to accommodate all nine of them. Makenzie, Mya and Issayah sat against the wall while Issayah's five cast mates sat on the opposite side. One seat was left empty for Chris.

It was karaoke night and the pizzeria was packed. Children anxiously ran back and forth from their parent's tables to the game room area dropping money in video games like Las Vegas slot machines. Waiters rushed around juggling pans of pizza and pitchers filled with beverages, barely avoiding accidents.

The smell from the kitchen made Makenzie's stomach growl like a pit bull ready to attack. She hadn't eaten since 6th period lunch and even then she only had an order of fries and a Pepsi. The waitress took their order twenty minutes ago so they still had another twenty minutes or more for their food. She hoped the pop she was sipping didn't spoil her appetite.

"What up, people?" Chris shouted with his hands in the air.

Everyone laughed as he made his way over. Issayah stood up on his feet, shook his hand then sat back down. Chris sat in the empty seat next to Mya. He flirted with her and then proceeded to tell everyone about the three point win over

Gloria Dotson-Lewis

Thornfeld High School.

When the pizza came, Makenzie had Issayah fix her a plate. She had to talk the group into ordering a veggie pizza. Since no one else really cared for it, they just ordered a small one. Her parents had introduced her to all types of vegetables at a very young age. Her friends tripped on her whenever she ate Brussels sprouts, beets or asparagus.

The hot slice of pizza burned her tongue as soon as she placed it in her mouth. She wanted to spit it back out but there was no way she was going out like that and have Robyn talking about it all over school. She tossed it around in her mouth then quickly picked up her cup of ice water and took a sip.

Makenzie thought Issayah's friends were all cool with the exception of Robyn and Paris, the only other girl who had come along from the drama team. They kept whispering and it was pissing Makenzie off. Robyn kept making small talk with Issayah about dumb stuff and Makenzie knew she was doing it to get under her skin. If her legs were just a little bit longer she would not so accidently kick her under the table.

"Mya, can you come to the bathroom with me?" Makenzie asked, interrupting her conversation with Chris.

"Yeah," she said, pushing herself away from the table. "I need to go anyway."

Makenzie walked in the first stall and locked the door. Mya entered the one two doors down. They washed their hands, applied fresh lip gloss and combed their hair back in place.

"Mya, is this chick trying to make me snap?" Makenzie said, after the tall silver haired lady walked out. "Do you see how she keeps talking to Issayah then whispering to ole girl?"

"Yeah. That is so freakin' rude. You're here with a group

and you keep whispering and snickering. I started to say something but I didn't want to mess up the celebration," Mya rolled her eyes.

"Girl, I was about to do the same thing. That's why I asked you to come in here with me. If I would have stayed there one more second it was going to come out."

"Well, just stay cool. Issayah is your man. She's the one that should be mad not you."

"You're right. Let's ignore these bust-downs and do some karaoke."

They walked out the bathroom and headed back to the table. Makenzie didn't have a view of the stage yet but she could tell the crowd's attention was directed that way. Heads were bobbing to *Bonnie and Clyde* by Jay-Z featuring Beyonce.

"Deg, that's the song I was going to try to get Issayah to do with me," Makenzie said, before smacking her lips.

Makenzie glanced at their table and noticed Issayah and Robyn missing and Paris smirking at her. She turned the corner of the room and a full view of the stage was before her eyes. When she saw Issayah and Robyn up there performing together she didn't have time to think before she reacted. She raced towards the stage, hurriedly squeezing past the crowd. She knocked a kid on his butt but kept moving. She didn't even hear the little boy's mother holler at her to watch where she was going.

She gripped Issayah's wrist and yanked him off the stage causing him to stumble forward. She cursed him out as she dragged him along behind her. Some customers looked on in confusion while others laughed. Robyn tried to keep singing to play things off but no one was paying her any attention so she stepped down.

"Deg, she gangster checked old boy." A guy in a Sox

baseball cap shouted out. The crowd burst out in laughter.

They stormed past their table of friends and out the front door to the parking lot.

"What the hell you doing on stage singing with Robyn? You gone play me like that right in my face!" Makenzie was screaming to the top of the mountains.

"It's karaoke. You act like you caught us in bed together. You're over reacting Makenzie, damn."

Makenzie was steaming like a pot of tea. She couldn't believe he was acting all innocent. He had just made her look stupid in front of a whole crowd of people and was now saying she was blowing things up.

"You probably are sleeping with her. She calling you outside of school and always up in your face. Tell me the truth Issayah! You not about to play me like a sucker," Makenzie shouted as she pushed him in the forehead.

"I think you better get out my face," Issayah said slapping Makenzie's hand from his face.

"Or what? Or what? What you gone do, huh?"

"Makenzie get out my face!" Issayah's nose flared in and out.

"I dare you to lay a hand on me."

Makenzie grabbed the gold chain that hung around Issayah's neck and pulled. It fell to the ground along with the microphone medallion dangling from it. Issayah shook his head at her then bent down to pick it up.

"I have never hit a female before in my life but I swear you're pushing me right now."

"I don't even know what you're mad for. You're the one out here trying to play me. If you wanna be with Robyn then go get with her and leave me out of it."

"Ain't nobody thinking about Robyn like that. If I wanted to be with her I would've came at her a long time ago,"

Issayah said as he stood up.

"Ya'll need to calm down. Why you letting that girl get to you? Issayah ain't thinking about no Robyn," Chris said as he and Mya walked across the parking lot in their direction.

"Well, he need to act like it. You gone wait til I go to the bathroom and pull some crap like that. Folks all laughing at me and stuff," she hollered at Issayah.

"Ain't nobody laughing at you, they laughing at me! You pulled me off that stage, remember?"

Makenzie struggled to get pass Chris but his 6'3" frame effortlessly held her back. She continued shouting and cursing as people looked on.

"Girl, let's go." Mya pulled her friend's arm. "Folks coming out here to be nosy," Mya said as she saw the crowd forming by the entrance.

When Chris saw that she had finally calmed down, he let down his guard and starting walking in Issayah's direction. Makenzie unzipped her purse and pulled out her keys as she headed towards her car. She lifted her arm and pulled it back behind her head. She moved it forward with all her strength, throwing it like a professional baseball player, hitting Issayah in his left cheek.

Issayah rushed toward Makenzie but Chris caught him by the shirt just in time.

"You know what? I don't have time for this b.s. It's over. Don't say nothing else to me, ever!"

"You'll be picking up the phone before I will," she shouted back.

Issayah jerked out of Chris's grip and walked towards his car, hopped in and drove off.

"What the hell just happened? Did my boy just drive off and leave me? I got dropped off up here so ya'll gone have to take me home?" Chris said shaking his head.

Gloria Dotson-Lewis

"Come on boy. You know we're not going to leave you out here stranded," Mya said grabbing his arm.

Makenzie went over to pick her keys up. As she walked back towards her car, she saw Robyn in the crowd looking at her, with a smile on her face.

chapter 14

Thanks for rolling with me to my grandma's house. I need to get some money from my dad and with you in the car waiting, he won't be able to hold me hostage," Makenzie said as Mya got in and closed the passenger's door.

"I know you're always calling your dad a deadbeat but man, I wish I had a dad like yours. He's always filling your pockets."

"No, you don't. All he's good for is his money, other than that, he's a deadbeat like I said."

"I hear that. I wouldn't trade my dad in for anybody but I just wish he wasn't so cheap," Mya laughed. "It's cool though, I wasn't doing nothing but waiting for Jeremih to retweet me and I can check that from my cellie. I'm trying to find out when he'll be coming home to the Chi."

"Yeah, right," Makenzie rolled her eyes. "Just don't let me get a call saying that you're locked up for stalking.

"Don't hate because I got a celebrity checking for me."

"Mya, he retweeted you once saying thanks for the love and that was like six months ago. When are you going to get over it?"

"That's the only one I told you about. What I didn't tell you is that he sent me his phone number and we talk on the phone every night before I go to sleep," Mya said.

"Whatever, crazy girl," Makenzie laughed at her friend.

"OMG, look at that chick standing on the bus stop. She is

giving dude the business. That looks like you checking Issayah the other night."

Makenzie stopped at the red light then directed her attention to the couple standing on the corner arguing. The girl was pretty. She reminded Makenzie of a young Keri Hilson just shorter with a thicker frame. The guy could pass for Lil Wayne's brother minus the gold teeth, dreadlocks and money. Mya cracked her window so they could hear the conversation.

"Ricky, the girl called and told me she's pregnant by you. Why would she lie?" The girl pushed him in the chest.

"Man I told you I only slept with that girl once and I used a condom. Shorty trying to trip me up. If she pregnant, it ain't mine."

"Where were ya'll at when you slept with her?"

"At her crib."

"So you never took her to your crib?"

"Never."

"Then tell me why she described your bedroom to me? I'm tired of your lies. You already had another baby on me and now this." Young Keri started crying and hitting her boyfriend as pedestrians looked on.

"Forget you if you don't believe me," he shouted before he pushed her to the ground and walked off.

Honkkk.

A white Range Rover sitting behind Makenzie startled her. She gawked through her rearview mirror then pulled off. The girl lifted herself off the ground and ran after him.

"That was a hot mess. She is too cute to let his ugly butt play her like a bust down," Makenzie said.

"She need to kick him to the moon and move on."

"Did you hear her? He already cheated on her before and she took him back even after he got another chick pregnant.

You Got Me Twisted

I couldn't do that one. The crazy part is, they got their business all in the streets; folks driving by watching."

"That don't sound familiar to you?" Mya looked at Makenzie.

"What? I know you're not talking about me and Issayah's situation. That was totally different. They was trying to play me right in my face and I wasn't having it. I might be a lot of things but a fool ain't one."

"Poor Issayah. He had no clue about your alter ego. She don't play."

"What you mean poor Issayah? Whose side are you on?" Makenzie looked over at Mya.

"Your side without a doubt but I think you went a little bit hard on Issayah."

"He had it coming point . . . blank . . . period."

So, you're telling me you don't regret the other night? You're not missing Issayah at all?"

"I ain't gone front. I miss him a little but he disrespected me so he needs to apologize."

"I feel you but maybe he feels like you disrespected him and need to apologize first."

"That won't happen."

Makenzie pulled into her grandmother's driveway, turned off the car then got out. "Wait here, I'll be right back."

"Okay."

She walked up the front stairs, rung the bell and waited. She heard the locks turning right before the door creaked open. Grandma P had on her favorite oversized flower night gown and slippers.

"Hi sweetie pie. How is my grandbaby doing?"

"I'm fine Grandma P. Smells like you're throwing down. What you cooking?" Makenzie said as she followed her into the kitchen.

"Oh, just some smothered chicken, rice and gravy, collard greens and sweet potatoes. You know there's plenty if you wanna stay."

"Maybe next time. My friend Mya is waiting for me outside. Is my dad here?"

"He ran out but he'll be right back. Sit down for a minute."

"Okay."

Makenzie was irritated. Her father was always pulling some last minute mess. He knew that she was coming by today at 3p.m. He should've been standing at the door with the money in hand waiting for her car to pull up. She had given him a script ahead of time so she could be in and out without having to be subjected to his lame conversations about nothing.

For the next fifteen minutes, Grandma P talked about growing up in Mobile, Alabama. Makenzie texted Mya five minutes ago to let her know what was taking so long. She was relieved when she heard the key unlocking the back door. If she thought she could get away with it, she would cuss her father out for making her wait.

The door flung open, Kalvin walked in. Makenzie's heart felt like it was about to burst through her chest as she locked eyes with him. A couple of months had passed since she saw him on Thanksgiving and she didn't even give a second thought that he'd still be around. He closed the door behind him. She immediately felt the urge to urinate and wanted to run but her body froze like a block of ice.

"Oh Kalvin honey, we thought you was your dad."

"It's just me granny."

"Well you're right on time to see your sister. Kalvin look how much your sister has grown."

Makenzie didn't say a word and she never took her eyes

off him. Kalvin smirked as he stared back.

"Wow, little sis, you've really become a beautiful young lady," He said as he looked her up and down while licking his lips. "We've lost a lot of time apart since I've been away. We need to do some catching up."

"That's a great idea. Maybe you two can plan a day to hang out," Grandma P said as she stirred her pot of greens.

"That's a good idea. I would love to come by the house and hang out like old times."

Makenzie's body shook as Kalvin moved closer. She fought back the tears trying to escape her eyes. She didn't want her grandmother to see her crying.

"I'm so proud of your brother. He helped to protect our country. He wrote me and sent me pictures all the time. I have an album full of nothing but pictures of him in different parts of the world," Grandma P said pulling her chicken out of the oven.

"Oh granny, you know you're my #1 girl. You kept me going while I was away. But, what I wanna know is why didn't you write me while I was away little sis?" He said, as he moved closer.

Makenzie jumped from her seat, knocking her chair to the floor. Grandma P turned around to see what the commotion was all about.

"I need to use the bathroom."

Makenzie ran from the kitchen to the bathroom down the hall. Once inside, she struggled to get her belt unbuckled as she danced in place. She sat down and released herself not a minute too soon.

Makenzie didn't care about the money anymore she just needed to get out of there. She exited the bathroom and ran out the front door without saying a word to anyone. As she ran down the front steps, she bumped into her father.

Gloria Dotson-Lewis

"Makenzie, are you okay?"

Makenzie didn't answer. She got in her vehicle, backed out the driveway and drove off.

chapter 15

Makenzie wiped her face with a warm cloth then looked at herself in the mirror. Her eyes were bloodshot red and her hair was scattered all over her head. She opened the medicine cabinet, took the Visine off the top shelf and squeezed two drops in each eye.

She had been extremely emotional today, which was a sign that her period was right around the corner. It could also be the whole Kalvin situation and the fact that she couldn't get Issayah out of her mind was a huge part of it. She played back the break up incident over and over in her head. Just a month ago they were eating off each other's plates and now her status was back to single on her Facebook page. She was angry with herself for not being able to contain her tears. Issayah played her for Robyn so he didn't deserve her. She wished none of it had happened but it did and now she and Issayah were over.

Makenzie abruptly stopped crying when she heard her cellular phone ring. She hoped that it was Issayah calling to apologize. She quickly dabbed her face dry, rushed to her room and picked up the phone from her bed. She didn't recognize the number and assumed he was calling her from someone else's phone.

"Hello," Makenzie said with an attitude.

"Hey cuz, I need to talk to you. Can I come through there?"

"Malkomb?" Makenzie questioned.

Gloria Dotson-Lewis

"Yeh, it's me. I'm about to come over."

"Boy, do you know what time it is? It's after midnight." Makenzie was irritated.

"And, I gotta tell you something and it can't wait," he said, through short, deep breaths.

"My mom is sleep so call me when you're outside so I can come open the door."

"Cool,"

Makenzie didn't have a clue what Malkomb needed to talk to her so urgently about. She tiptoed to the living room and sat on the couch as she waited on his call. He sounded as if he had just run a marathon. She wondered if someone was after him and he was bringing trouble to her house. Maybe she should've told him not to come by. Makenzie's phoned sounded. She picked up and headed to the door.

"What is so important that it couldn't wait until tomorrow?" Makenzie whispered as she let Malkomb in then closed the door behind them.

"We got him," he said in an excited soft voice.

"Got who? Malkomb, I hope you ain't putting me and my momma in danger by coming over here after doing something dumb. You my cousin and I love you but I don't want no parts of any gang mess," Makenzie fussed.

Makenzie had heard that Malkomb was in a gang. He was never a tough kid while growing up. Makenzie believed it was more about filling that void that his father left behind. But, whatever was going on, she didn't want any parts of it.

"We've been following him for a couple of days but he was always with someone. When we saw his car outside of the 50 Yard Line on 75th Street, we sat in the car and waited for him to come out. He walked out with some guys he used to hang with back in the day," Malkomb pounded his right fist in his left palm as he replayed the incident in his head.

You Got Me Twisted

Makenzie didn't have a clue what Malkomb was talking about. She hoped he wasn't about to tell her something she would later have to testify in front of a jury about.

"We followed him back to Grandma P's house," he said as he looked in Makenzie's eyes.

"Grandma P's? Are you talking about Kalvin?" She covered her mouth.

"Makenzie, I had to get him for what he did to you. I couldn't let him get away with that. He's sitting over Grandma P's acting all innocent and stuff. All up in Grandma P's face like he's the perfect grandson. I had to get him."

"What did you do Malkomb? Makenzie's voice escalated.

"Shhhh."

"Tell me. What did you do?"

"It was late. Wasn't no parking spots near the house and your dad and Grandma P's car was in the driveway. Kalvin had to park way down the street. Me and my boy CJ let him get out of his car then we got out. I told him I knew about what he did to you but he denied it. He started calling you a liar and a freak and it pissed me off," Malkomb huffed.

"I told you not to say a word," Makenzie cried. "You promised."

"I'm sorry. I didn't plan on saying anything but you shoulda saw how he was around there talking about all the places he traveled and the metals he received. The family sitting over there eating that mess up but be talking about me behind my back like I'm the worst person in the world," Malkomb said as veins popped out of his forehead.

"I can't believe this is happening. That's why I kept it to myself all these years," Makenzie said, shaking her head. "What did you do to him?"

"He was talking all this mess, thought he was bad cause

103

he was in the military. CJ handed me the bat he had behind his back and I played ball. I beat him real good for you cuz. I could've killed him but he's fam so I let him live."

"What? You didn't do it for me, you did it for you. I told you not to tell anyone and this is what you do? Now the whole family will probably find out!"

"He ain't gon tell nobody. If he tell, he have to explain why I did it and I know he don't want to bring that up."

"You better be right or else I'll never speak to you again," Makenzie swore.

"Makenzie, who are you talking to down there?" Rhonda called from the top of the stairs.

"Nobody mom. It's the television."

"Well, turn it off and go to bed."

"Okay," she answered. "You gotta go before my mom come down here."

"Okay, okay. Don't worry. No one will find out. I'll holla at you later," Malkomb said, as he creeped out the front door.

"I can't believe this is happening to me," Makenzie cried as she leaned her back against the front door and slid to the floor.

chapter 16

Makenzie sat on Dr. Reid's sofa with one leg relaxing across the other, biting her nails. She had a lot on her mind and felt like her head was going to explode. She needed to talk to someone and Dr. Reid was the only person who she felt she could be truthful to without being judged and she didn't have to worry about it getting out.

"Hi Makenzie. How are you today?" Dr. Reid asked as she took a sip from her Starbucks coffee cup.

"Okay, I guess," Makenzie said as she looked at the floor.

"You don't sound okay. Did something happen this past week?"

Makenzie bit her jaws and closed her eyes to fight back her tears. She was tired of crying and this morning, as she looked in the mirror, she told herself today she would be strong. But, as soon as Dr. Reid started talking, she felt herself breaking.

"Makenzie? Can you tell me what happened?"

"I told a cousin about a secret that I've been holding on to for years; something that happened when I was younger. I told him not to tell anyone but he did and now I'm afraid other family members may find out about it."

"How does that make you feel?"

"I just wish I would've never told him. I kept it to myself all these years and when I finally tell someone, this happens. I am so stupid," Makenzie said, as she shook her head.

"You're not stupid Makenzie. It had to be difficult for

you to harbor a secret all by yourself so young. Maybe it was time for you to share the secret with someone. Do you think your cousin told the other person out of spite?"

"No, I'm sure he thought he was doing the right thing. He's always been protective of me growing up. I'm just afraid that it may get out. My mom, what if she finds out?" Makenzie's eyes began to water.

"Have you ever thought about telling your mother what happened?"

"Yeah, after my dad left. I wanted to tell her but I just couldn't bring myself to do it. I didn't want my dad to get in trouble. I still loved him and I just thought things would eventually get better between us. I wanted so bad for things to go back to the way they were."

"I see. Would you like to talk about it?" Dr. Reid asked, trying carefully to get Makenzie to open up about her secret.

"No, I can't," she cried.

"It's okay, whenever you're ready we can talk about it." Dr. Reid handed Makenzie a box of tissue. "Has anything else happened lately that you want to talk about?" She asked, changing the subject.

"Well yeah," she uttered. "Me and my boyfriend Issayah broke up."

"What happened?"

"He was disrespecting me in front of a room full of people in Beggers so I had to check him. When we got outside he threatened to hit me and started talking all that yaya which made me snap so I jacked him up. "

"How do you feel about that?"

"I have mixed feelings, I guess. I miss him but at the same time I can't let him dog me out like that. If he called me to apologize, I would probably make him suffer a little but I would forgive him."

Dr. Reid made notes that Makenzie was aggressive and physically abusive, particularly towards male figures in her life. From the sessions she's had with Makenzie so far, she suspected that this secret she spoke of was related. She knew from experience that she may not get her patient to open up to her but she would try to show her the possible connection and try to help her manage her anger issues.

"Sounds like you have a lot going on all at one time. I'm sure your emotions are all over the place. And, it's okay for you to feel angry when someone upsets you but it's not okay to physically harm someone or for someone to harm you out of anger. There are ways that you can work on coping with your anger but first I think it's important to recognize the signs. Can you tell me what happens to your body when you get angry?"

"Well, sometimes my stomach gets upset when I'm really mad."

"Ok, that's good. What else?" Dr. Reid asked as she wrote down Makenzie's responses.

"I can feel my chest getting tight sometimes and I bite my jaws," Makenzie said after some thought.

"Good, good. Now, those are all physical symptoms but some people also experience mental signs as well, like problems concentrating and thoughts of doing harm."

Makenzie diverted her eyes to the floor. She knew she was guilty of most of the things Dr. Reid was discussing.

"Some people also yell and curse while others withdraw from others. What's important is that you recognize the signs so that you can begin to control your anger instead of letting your emotions take over which can be dangerous. It's going to take a lot of practice but it can be done."

"What about if people just stop pushing my buttons and getting on my nerves? Sometimes people get what they deserve," Makenzie responded.

"Unfortunately, we can't change other people Makenzie but we can change how we respond to them. What does fighting someone really solve when it's all said and done? Have you known it to change anything?"

"No, not really but people know not to mess with me."

"Well I'm sure you can get that across in a more positive manner. There are several things you can do to control your anger. One simple way is to just walk away and leave that person standing there. If there is something that needs to be addressed, you can deal with it later when you're calm. Counting to ten can help to calm you. You can also talk to someone who you're not angry with about how you're feeling. This can help to relieve some anxiety. You can also write about it. When you get stuff out it's like a weight lifted off of you."

Makenzie was listening closely to Dr. Reid, nodding her head at times in agreement. She knew she overreacted at times and she also knew she had never once thought about just walking away. She always felt like she had to fight to get her point across.

"I'm going to give you an assignment. I want you to write a letter to your father expressing your feelings towards him. You can talk about anything that's on your mind and it can be as long or as short as you want it to be. You can write it and tear it up or you can give it to him. That is solely up to you. I think it would help for you to get some things out. Is that okay?"

"Yeah, I can do that," Makenzie said as she took a deep breath.

"Good. I also want your mother to join us next week. So, I think it would be a good idea for you to write down some things you would like to talk to her about as well."

"Why does she have to come?" Makenzie frowned.

"I think you're making wonderful progress and family therapy can help to advance you even further."

"Will you be telling her stuff I told you in private?"

Makenzie didn't want her mother to know any more than she had to about her personal business. She would rather take her chances walking into a lion's den at the local zoo. Makenzie knew that her mother would overreact or start trying to fix things with her stupid advice.

"No, we won't discuss anything you don't want to."

"Good," Makenzie said, relieved.

chapter 17

The Journalism Department was right down the hall from the auditorium. Makenzie started taking the long route to keep from possibly running into Issayah but today she was late for a meeting so she couldn't avoid walking in that direction. It was after hours and most of the students were gone for the day. She took a deep breath after making it past the entrance without being seen. Makenzie rushed in the small room, disrupting the meeting already in progress.

"I'm glad that you could join us Ms. Pierce," Mr. Walters, head of the journalism department, remarked.

"Sorry, I was speaking to my Calculus teacher about an upcoming exam and lost track of time."

"Well, to bring you up to speed, we are brainstorming some ideas for the next issue. We have quite a few topics and need to narrow them down. As the Managing Editor we need your assistance in determining which one should be the lead story," Mr. Walters said.

"Okay, so what do we have so far?" Makenzie said, jumping in.

"There have been quite a few school shootings on college campus' lately. I think maybe that's an issue we could cover," A petite girl with dark shades spoke up.

"That's a great idea, Yolanda, but I think it's a huge topic to research in such a short period of time. We don't even know if our school has a protocol in place if something like that were to happen here. But, it's something we can look into for a later time," Makenzie said. "What else do we have?"

"Well, we could cover the wrestling team who is headed to the state finals," James jumped in. "Or we could do a story on Mr. Moore, the biology teacher. He's always telling stories about his war days. We can let the students see, through his story, some of the things they face during war and what happens when they return home."

"That's a great idea, James. Write a little information on each topic and what you would like to cover and we'll consider them."

"What about date rape? I was watching this program where this seventeen year old girl went out on a date with a guy who slipped something in her drink. His parents weren't home so he took her back to his house and took advantage of her," Mya chimed in."

"I have a friend that actually went through that. I may be able to get an interview for us," LaTavia, one of the newspaper reporters volunteered.

Mya's idea made Makenzie cringe. Her stomach did somersaults as an image of Kalvin holding her down, forcing himself on her, flashed across her mind. She stood up and walked over to the opened window and took a deep breath.

"Makenzie, did you hear me? What do you think?" Mya asked.

"Umm . . . yeah, I heard you. Can you guys excuse me for a minute? I need to go to the washroom."

Makenzie walked out the door before anyone could respond. She was startled when she looked up and saw Robyn and her friend Paris coming out of the ladies' room. She did not feel like dealing with the whole drama thing right now but she knew from the look on their faces it was coming.

"Well, look who we have here," Robyn said. "I haven't seen you since that night at Beggers. How are you feeling?"

"Please, like you care."

"I do. That night must have been hard on you. I mean I've never been dumped in front of so many people before but I can image how embarrassing it must have been for you," Robyn smirked.

"Robyn, I'm not in the mood so you need to keep it moving for real," Makenzie said as her chest tightened. She started counting to ten in her head.

"I'm just saying, who does that? You pulled Issayah off the freakin' stage in front of all those people making him look like a punk. You didn't expect him to dump you? I told you he and I are just friends and that you didn't have to feel so insecure about our friendship. But--""

"Look trick, I don't have anything to be insecure about. I see right through you even if Issayah don't. I know what you were on that night at Beggar's."

"I don't know what you're talking about," Robyn said as she hunched her shoulders.

"Robyn, he's not around. You don't have to pretend. Just be real, you want Issayah for yourself," Makenzie said.

"Yeah, you're right, I do like Issayah. And you made it so easy for me to come between you two. You let me know how jealous you were when you had him call me on the phone that day tripping. So, I waited until you went to the bathroom and made my move." Robyn grinned then turned around to give her friend high-five.

"I hope it was worth it because it's about to cost you a beat down."

Makenzie snatched Robyn's ponytail and slammed her

into the lockers like a rag doll. Robyn let out a squeal then grabbed the back of her head as it bounced off the metal surface. As Makenzie tightened her grip on Robyn's hair with her right hand, she balled up her left fist and started wildly swinging at her face. She landed two blows; one to the mouth, the other to the right eye before Robyn blocked her face with both arms.

"Leave her alone," Paris yelled at Makenzie from a distance.

"Shut up before I get you next," Makenzie said as she stopped hitting Robyn to point at Paris.

Robyn quickly took a piece of Makenzie's dangling hair in her hand and twisted it around her finger to get a tight grip. She quickly punched her in the jaw with her free hand before Makenzie realized what was happening. They wrestled to the floor, Makenzie landing on top.

"I can't stand . . . females like you . . . always scheming . . . on getting somebody's man . . . " Makenzie said as she sat on Robyn's midsection talking between licks.

Makenzie really liked Issayah and hated Robyn for coming between them. It felt like all the men in her life that meant a lot left; her father, Malkomb, when he went away to jail, and now Issayah. She wanted to draw blood.

"Makenzie, chill! What are you doing?" Issayah said, as he rushed up the hall.

Makenzie dropped her hands and turned in Issayah's direction. "I told you. She just admitted to me that she wants you for yourself."

"So you're beating her up?"

"She planned the whole thing at Beggars. She did it to come between us," Makenzie said as she lifted herself from Robyn and stood to her feet. She rubbed the jaw that Robyn hit her in.

"I guess she told you to come pull me off the stage too?" Issayah sarcastically questioned.

"No but she knew I would get mad. It's her fault everything turned out the way it did."

"She's lying. I had no clue she would get upset over us doing karaoke together," Robyn said as she sat up.

"You lying trick," Makenzie said as she charged Robyn knocking her back to the floor. Issayah ran over and attempted to pull Makenzie off Robyn as Paris tried to pry their hands from each other's hair.

Mya peeked out the door to see if Makenzie was coming down the hall. When she saw the commotion, she ran towards them. She helped to separate the girls and tried to get Makenzie to calm down.

"You can't go around hitting folks every time they make you mad," Issayah said as he pulled Robyn from the floor and stood in front of her.

Makenzie felt betrayed by Issayah again. She couldn't believe he was standing in front of Robyn protecting and defending her.

"If folks don't wanna get hit they need to quit talking so much. It's just that simple."

"Makenzie let's go. We need to get back to our meeting," Mya said, grabbing Makenzie's arm.

"Yeah, let's go before I hurt somebody for real," Makenzie said as she walked away with Mya. Dr. Reid suddenly popped in her head.

Maybe I should have just walked away and avoided the situation like Dr. Reid said. Naw, that trick deserved that.

chapter 18

Makenzie sat silent as she looked out the window of her mother's Land Rover. It was a frigid January morning outside and snow flurries filled the sky. She was nervous about the whole family therapy thing. She really didn't have a good feeling about her mother being in on her sessions. She decided she wouldn't be talking about much with her mother there.

They pulled up to the rust two flat building in the Hyde Park neighborhood and parked. As they entered the structure, a tall stocky man in a grey suit held the door opened for them. They were fifteen minutes early so they signed in and sat in the waiting room. Makenzie picked up a Sister2Sister Magazine with R&B singer Monica on the cover with her new NBA husband Shannon Brown.

Dr. Reid emerged from her office in a black pants suit with three inch pumps. Her short spiked hair was dyed an almond brown that matched her skin complexion perfectly.

"Good morning ladies, you can come back now."

They stood up and followed her into the room. Rhonda sat down with perfect posture on the right side of the couch. Makenzie settled on the far left side leaning her body on the armrest. Dr. Reid smiled as she took her place across from them.

"How are you ladies this morning?"

"Fine," they chimed.

"Well, I wanted us all to meet because Makenzie and I don't have a lot of sessions left and I wanted to discuss her progress."

"Okay," Rhonda said.

"We can also discuss whatever is on your minds today. I want to start by first saying that Makenzie is an intelligent, candid young lady with a big heart. She started out a little rough around the edges but as we got to know each other she has let her guard down," Dr. Reid paused and smiled at Makenzie.

"I feel that Makenzie has evolved over the months but still has some work to do. She has completed several assignments which has helped her to express her feelings about a few issues which is a great start to self improvement. She sometimes becomes physical when she gets really upset and that's what we need to continue to work on. I think with some more Cognitive-Behavioral Strategies, she'll be on her way."

"Cognitive what?" Rhonda asked.

"Oh I'm sorry. Cognitive-Behavioral Strategies are approaches that are used to aid in replacing negative thinking with more rational thoughts so that positive behavior can begin to occur. For example, I'll give her different scenarios to address, for instance, a girl at school laughs at Makenzie's outfit and she becomes really upset. We would discuss ways she could respond without getting physical. One way may be stopping and thinking before reacting or moving to another area to avoid the situation all together."

"Oh okay, that sounds like a great idea. Maybe it can help her at home to with how she treats me," Rhonda said as she turned and looked at Makenzie.

"Huh, here we go," Makenzie said.

You Got Me Twisted

"How would you say Makenzie treats you?" Dr. Reid asked.

"No matter what I do for her it's never enough. She's always talking back. She yells and tells me I make her sick and she can't stand me."

"How does that make you feel?"

"It hurts. She's my only child and I hate that we're not close."

"Why do you think that is?"

"I think she's mad at the world because her father and I split up. They were really close and she hasn't been the same since then."

"Whatever," Makenzie mumbled as she rolled her eyes and shifted her body.

"I'm sorry your father left Makenzie, but I don't think it's fair that you take it out on me. I've been letting you get away with stuff because I know how much the divorce affected you. You stopped talking for a while and you started peeing in the bed. Then, when you started getting older, you didn't want anything to do with your father. I didn't want your relationship with him to suffer because he fell out of love with me but I didn't know what to do." Rhonda got choked up as tears began to fill her eyes.

"He didn't fall out of love with you," Makenzie said.

"You're too young to understand," Rhonda said.

"I understand more than you know. Dad didn't leave because he fell out of love with you. He left because of Kalvin," Makenzie said as she bit a nail from her hand.

"Kalvin? What are you talking about?"

"Who is Kalvin, sweetie?" Dr. Reid asked.

"My half brother."

"He's my ex-husband's older son. He went away to the military four years ago. I don't understand what he has to do with this."

"Can you explain to us what your brother has to do with your father leaving you and your mom?" Dr. Reid gently pried.

Makenzie cried uncontrollably. She was tired of carrying this secret and needed to get it off her chest. She opened up to her cousin Malkomb but had only told him part of it. She knew it was time to tell it all.

"Kalvin lived in Michigan with his mom but used to come visit every summer. If we weren't at our house, we were at Grandma P's. I looked up to him. My dad would get a break when he was around because I would follow him around instead of my dad. I thought he was the coolest big brother in the world. Until . . ." Makenzie grabbed some Kleenex from the box on the side table and blew her nose.

Concern covered Rhonda's face as she looked at Makenzie in shock. "Until what Makenzie?"

"What happened, Makenzie?" Dr. Reid asked a second time.

"One night, when I was twelve, my parents went out to dinner. They left Kalvin in charge just like they always did. We were in his room listening to music and playing video games. Out of nowhere, he leaned over and squeezed one of my breasts."

"Stop nasty."

"Why? You let Mike across the street touch you. I saw you kissing him and letting him touch you in the garage yesterday. I was looking out the window."

"You're lying. He was helping me fix my bike tire."

"I saw you. I even took pictures. I'm going to show them to dad and your mom unless you do what I say."

"Please don't show them. What do you want me to do?"

"Take off your clothes and lay down and you better not

tell anyone."

"I can still see it so vividly in my mind. I remember everything in that room. I even remember the smell of Unforgivable cologne coming from his body. That smell still makes me sick to the stomach," Makenzie cried as she remembered the details.

"Oh my gosh." Rhonda whispered.

"I'm so sorry, honey. Did you tell anyone?"

"I was too afraid. I felt guilty for what I did with Mike. I was scared that my parents would find out and hate me. I told Kalvin I didn't want to do it but he wouldn't listen. I cried and asked him to stop but he just told me to shut up. It hurt so bad but he wouldn't stop. When he was done, I felt dirty. I remember praying that it would never happen again and no one would find out. It was like he turned into a demon. He wasn't the same person I used to know. I started avoiding him around the house. My parents noticed the change and would ask me was I okay but I would tell them I was fine."

"So this happened more than once."

"Three times."

Rhonda covered her mouth and wept. She was too shocked to speak.

"Now, you mentioned your father left because of Kalvin. Did you eventually tell him?"

"No. One day Kalvin forced himself on me while my parents were at work. He called me from my room into the living room where he was watching television. The TV must have been loud because we didn't hear the door open. My dad wasn't feeling good so he left work early to come home. He saw my brother on top of me with his pants down and lost it. He started punching him in the face and chest. He slammed him into the fireplace and kicked him when he was down. I remember thinking he was going to kill him. He sent him upstairs to pack his bag. While he was upstairs my dad helped me get dressed then took me into his arms and held me tight."

"Are you okay sweetheart?"

"No, daddy! He made me do it. I told him to stop but he wouldn't."

"I know sweetheart. You won't have to worry about him anymore. Daddy's going to take care of him for you but you have to promise that this will be our little secret. You can't tell your mom or anyone okay?"

Makenzie was crying and didn't say anything.

"You love daddy don't you?"

Makenzie nodded her head.

"You trust me don't you?"

"Yes, daddy."

"Then promise me you won't tell anybody about what Kalvin did to you."

"I promise."

"How did you feel about your father making you keep everything a secret?" Dr. Reid asked.

"I loved my dad and I trusted him to make the pain go away so it wasn't hard to keep our secret. But, things changed. He couldn't look me in the face anymore. He started avoiding me. He wouldn't come home until I was already in the bed sleep. He started drinking and he and my mom started arguing all the time. He hated me for what happened and there was nothing I could do to take it back," Makenzie rested her face in her hands and wept.

"Sweetheart, why didn't you come to me?" Rhonda said as she touched Makenzie's shoulder.

"I didn't want dad to get in trouble at first. Then, later I wanted to tell you but you seemed more concerned about me forgiving my dad than anything else. I hated you for that."

"I'm so sorry. I didn't know what you were going through. I love you more than anything in the world. I thought if you and your dad's relationship could be repaired you would be happy like you use to be."

Dr. Reid grabbed some tissue and handed it to Makenzie. Rhonda took her in her arms and gave her a much needed embrace.

"I feel like all the men in my life have hurt me," Makenzie sat up and dried her eyes.

"How does that make you feel?" Dr. Reid inquired.

"I feel sad, angry, weak, worthless; all of those things. I feel like I have to fight to stay in control. I can't let anyone else have that power over me anymore. I'll fight anyone who tries to hurt or disrespect me or anyone who tries to come between me and someone I love."

"I think that's enough for one day. Makenzie, I'd like to talk to your mom in private for just a moment. Can you wait in the lobby?"

"Yes."

"I would still like for you to write a letter to your father expressing your feelings to him if that's okay. You don't have to give it to him if you don't want. This is more for you than anyone."

"Ok, Dr. Reid. I'll try."

"Have a good week Makenzie," Dr. Reid said as Makenzie left the office."

"Ms. Pierce, I know you're in a state of disbelief right now. It has to be very heartbreaking to know that your daughter has been dealing with something like this for all these years. You're going to go through a lot of emotional distress too and I want to open my doors to you for therapy as well."

"Thanks, I'm sure I'll need it," she said as she dabbed her eyes with Kleenex.

"I wanted to also talk to you in private about the legal issues that must take place. A crime has been committed against Makenzie and it is my job to report it. You ex-husband and stepson maybe brought up on charges. I didn't want to tell Makenzie about this right now because she's dealing with a lot but I wanted you to know."

"Do what you have to do. Those bastards need to be locked up for doing this to my baby."

chapter 19

Makenzie forced herself to sit up on the edge of her bed. She had already hit the snooze button three times on her alarm clock in the last twenty minutes. Her track coach instructed her and her teammates to run five miles every other morning at 6 a.m. for the next two weeks as part of their conditioning for pre-season. She usually met up with a couple of her teammates but today she needed to be alone. Her mother would be upset if she knew she was running by herself but she had a lot on her mind and needed to clear her head. Besides, she had her mace and whistle ready for anyone who approached her the wrong way.

Her legs felt like a ton of bricks as she walked to the washroom to release herself. She washed her face and brushed her teeth then went back to her room to change. She removed her PINK pajama bottoms and matching t-shirt then threw on her blue and white track jogging pants and pull over hoodie sweat shirt. Makenzie stepped outside to the driveway where she stretched for five minutes before taking off down the street.

The cool air hit her in the face as she jogged south on State Street. The morning sky mimicked her mood, gray and void of sunlight. The neighborhood was quiet except for an occasional passing car and her neighbor's barking dog. As she ran in silence, thoughts of her last session with Dr. Reid dominated her brain.

Gloria Dotson-Lewis

The meeting was extremely overwhelming and brought out a lot of feelings she hadn't dealt with in years. Makenzie was relieved that her mother knew everything and she no longer had to lie or make excuses about why she didn't want to have a relationship with her father. But, what she did worry about was her other family members reactions now that the secret was out. Everyone knew Grandma P was crazy about her oldest grandson Kalvin. She was always showing pictures of him in his Army uniform and talking about how proud she is of him for serving his country. She wondered if Grandma P would believe her or Kalvin's side of the story. And would everyone treat her differently?

Makenzie started walking when she reached her block, allowing her body time to cool down. She stretched her arms and legs another five minutes before she entered the house. She stripped, hopped in the shower and let the warm water run over her body. She wrapped a towel around her torso, patted herself dry and changed back into her pajamas.

It was Wednesday, late start day. Makenzie didn't have to be at school until 9:45am. She took a notebook and pen from her desk top then lay across her bed. When she flipped it open, her eyes were immediately directed to the big heart, with Makenzie loves Issayah in the center, that was drawn on the inside cover. She drew it before the break up and thought about whiting it out then decided she'd leave it there just in case he came to his senses.

Makenzie must have picked up the same pen over a hundred times in the last two days to write her father the letter Dr. Reid suggested. She knew Dr. Reid's intentions were good but she really didn't see how writing this letter would make her feel any better.

"Come on Makenzie, just do it. It's not like you're going to actually give it to him anyway," she said out loud to herself. "Ok, here goes nothing."

Dear Mr. Pierce, A.K.A Sperm Donor,
I hate you! I can't even look at you without hate in my heart for you. How can anyone love someone so much then turn around and despise them? Well, that's how I feel about you.
A dad is supposed to protect his daughter but you failed. There's not a person on earth I loved more than you and you let me down. One of the worst things that could happen to a young girl happened to me and your reaction was to leave me to deal with it on my own. Where were you when I cried out in the middle of the night because I was having nightmares? Where were you when I started wetting the bed like a little girl because I was too afraid to go to the bathroom, thinking Kalvin was in the halls waiting on me?
Your son raped me and you, my father, swept it under the rug like nothing ever happened. You made me promise not to tell a soul and I didn't. I thought things would go back to normal after Kalvin left but after that day things were never the same again. I lost my father and my best friend that day.
You used to be a father any girl would love to have then you became a deadbeat dad who came around smelling like a bum on the streets. You missed some of the most important moments of my life. You weren't in the stands when I won the track state championship trophy and you even missed my 8th grade graduation. Do you have a clue how that made me feel?
I have so many great memories before that day but they've been overshadowed by all the bad days that followed. The pain, guilt and memories still haunt me to this day. I don't care if I ever see you again. You could die today and I wouldn't attend your funeral. You mean nothing to me

Gloria Dotson-Lewis

and I'll never ever forgive you.
  A Fatherless Child

Makenzie laid the pen down, closed the tear stained notebook and pushed her chair away from the desk. She strolled over to her window, looked out at the falling snowflakes and took a deep breath. Dr. Reid was right; she did feel a little better. She kept most of those memories bottled up for years; trying to convince herself that they didn't affect her but now she knew otherwise. Maybe one day she'd have the nerve to actually give it to him.

Maybe then he'll feel my pain.

chapter 20

akenzie headed down the stairs after straightening her bedroom and finishing her homework. Although it was only seven in the evening she had already showered and changed into her sleepwear. She was tired after a strenuous track practice and just wanted to relax the rest of the night.

She walked in the kitchen, opened the refrigerator and took a green apple from the bottom compartment. She removed a small saucer out the upper cabinet, grabbed a steak knife and walked into the living room. After grabbing the remote from the ottoman she flopped down on her favorite spot on the sofa.

Makenzie sliced her apple in six sections and placed the knife on the side table. She searched the channels, stopping at Damon Wayans and Tisha Campbell in My Wife and Kids. It was her favorite show and she watched the reruns over and over whenever she came across them. Every episode made her laugh like it was her very first time seeing them.

Makenzie huffed in irritation when she heard the doorbell ring. Her mother had a habit of ringing the bell just because she didn't feel like using her keys to unlock the door. She took a bite from the slice of apple she was holding in her hand then placed the remainder back on the plate. She lifted herself from her seat, marched through the kitchen, unlocked the back door then pulled it open.

"Why don't you ever use . . ." Makenzie stopped midsentence when she saw Kalvin looking down at her. He was wearing black from head to toe. His lean, 6ft 3in frame stood there holding the outer security door open with one hand. Makenzie tried to force the door shut but Kalvin shoved it open forcing his way inside.

"What are you doing here? I'm going to call the police if you don't get out," Makenzie's voiced trembled.

"You know exactly why I'm here," Kalvin said as he slammed the door shut.

Makenzie's heart was beating so fast she thought it was going to burst out of her chest. She blindly backed up as he moved closer to her. She glanced towards the steps then back at Kalvin trying to figure out if she had enough time to make an escape to her room so she could lock the door and call for help. But, he watched her eyes and walked in that direction to the block the stairway.

"Why did you have to go bringing up the past. Dad said you'd take it to the grave and never tell anyone if I went away!" Kalvin cracked his knuckles as he starred at Makenzie.

"Malkomb was the only person I told. He promised not to say a word. I . . . I didn't know . . ."

"Well he did." Kalvin shouted. "Malkomb and his boy jumped me and it's your fault. Had you kept your big mouth shut everything would be cool!"

Makenzie looked in his eyes and saw nothing but pure evil. She had nowhere to escape. She was shaking like a bobble head on a dashboard as he continued to approach her.

"Kalvin, please . . . " Makenzie cried.

"Please what!" He yelled as he lunged towards her, grabbing her upper arms. "This whole thing is your fault. Why couldn't you just leave this mess alone? I suffered enough for it. I spent four years of my life in the military because of you and my dad hates me to this day because of what he thinks I did to his precious daughter. I didn't have to force you. You wanted it. You didn't even put up a fight."

Makenzie couldn't believe that he was blaming the whole thing on her. She was the victim, not him. Her fear was suddenly replaced by anger. She twisted her body back and forth, attempting to release herself from his grip.

"I was twelve and I was scared. I didn't want you to touch me. I hate you, I hate you," Makenzie shouted then spit in Kalvin's face.

He slapped her left cheek then wrestled her down on the couch and sat on top of her, holding her down with his weight.

"Relax, I just want to play catch up with my little sister. I see you've grown up and out," Kalvin said as looked down at Makenzie's breast while licking his lips. He held her small wrists with one hand. He tugged at her tank top with his free hand, ripping it down the middle.

"Get off of me," she yelled, as she continued to struggle. She finally twisted her right wrist out of his hand and socked him in the nose with all her might sending blood racing down his face.

"You stupid slut," Kalvin shouted as he let go of Makenzie's other wrist to grip his nose.

Kalvin placed his arm up to his nose to use his shirt sleeve to try to stop the blood flow. While he was occupied, Makenzie lifted her arms over her head. Her finger tips searched the end table for her knife. She felt the pointy tip but couldn't get a grip on it. She pushed her body back a couple of inches, picked up the knife and jabbed Kalvin in the upper right side of his chest.

His eyes bucked wide as he gasped in shock. He climbed

off Makenzie and stumbled to the floor. Makenzie sat upright and grabbed her legs, holding herself in a fetal position. She stared at Kalvin as she sat there rocking herself in place. He gasped as he took each breath.

The door bell rang, snapping Makenzie out of her state of shock.

"Mom, help!" Makenzie cried.

She heard the door open and footsteps heading her way. When she looked up her father was standing there. He looked at her and then at Kalvin lying on the floor with the knife still standing upright.

"What did you do?" Walter shouted as he ran towards Kalvin. "Did you call 9-1-1?" He asked Makenzie.

She didn't say a word. She just kept rocking back and forth.

"Kalvin, can you hear me? Don't you die, you hear me! Kalvin!" Walter pulled his cell phone out of his pocket and kneeled over his son. He dialed 9-1-1 and hit the call button.

"Yes, can I get an ambulance? My son has been stabbed and he looks like he's losing a lot of blood! Yes, he's still breathing but barely."

Walter sat there talking to Kalvin while holding his hand trying to keep him from going to sleep. Sirens could be heard coming up the block a few minutes later. Walter Pierce told Makenzie to open the front door but she didn't move. He jumped to his feet, opened the front door and saw a police car pulling up in front of the house. A short, petite female officer got out the driver side and ran towards the house with her hand on her holster. Her partner, a stocky older man with thin framed glasses followed behind her.

"I'm Officer Blair and this is Officer Scott. Can you tell us what happened here?" The male officer asked as he kneeled down next to them.

"Where is the ambulance? My son is dying. Can you tell the paramedics to hurry up?"

"Sir calm down. They're on the way," Officer Blair said with his palms raised towards Walter, trying to calm him.

"That's easy for you to say. It's not your son that's lying here."

Officer Scott walked over to Makenzie and sat down. "Can you tell me what happened sweetie? Did you stab him?"

Rhonda pulled up seconds before the ambulance. She jumped out the car leaving the door wide open.

"Makenzie!" She hollered as she ran through the door looking around for her daughter. She glanced down at Kalvin and her ex as she made her way to Makenzie on the couch. Rhonda stood over her and embraced her face with both hands.

"Are you okay?" She asked ignoring the police officer. Makenzie nodded yes, and then tightly hugged her mother around the waist, wailing uncontrollably.

"What happened? What are they doing in my house? Walter, what the hell are you and that rapist doing in my house?" Rhonda hollered at her ex-husband.

He ignored her and kept talking to Kalvin, trying to keep him from going to sleep. The paramedics entered the house, rushing over to Kalvin. They placed an oxygen mask over his face then packed gauze around the knife to help stop the bleeding. They rolled him to one side, slid a flat board under him and lifted him up on a wheeled cot. They pushed him towards the van with Makenzie's father following closely behind.

"He stopped breathing," One of the paramedics shouted from the front porch.

Makenzie's eyes grew as wide as a satellite dish as she

saw the middle aged man tilt Kalvin's head back, blow two breaths into his mouth then touch the side of his neck to check for a pulse. Next, he intertwined his fingers, placed his hands on Kalvin's chest and pumped on the center several times trying to avoid the area of the knife.

Makenzie chewed on her nails as her body trembled. She dropped her head to her knees to cover her face. When she looked back up they were sliding him in the vehicle. Walter got in behind them and rode to the hospital with his son.

"We need to know what happened here," the male officer walked over. "Did you stab that young man?"

Makenzie looked up at her mother for help.

"She was defending herself. He wasn't supposed to be in my house!" Rhonda cried out.

"I'm sorry but we're going to have to take her down to the police station. If it was self defense, they'll release her but we have to take her in. Can you go get your daughter some clothes to change into?"

"Mom no! I don't wanna go to jail." Makenzie yelled as she squeezed her mother even tighter.

Rhonda held on to Makenzie for a few seconds before releasing her. She was scared for her daughter but didn't want Makenzie to see her break down so she fought back the tears that were forming in her eyes. She kissed her forehead, told her she loved her and that everything would be okay. Rhonda went upstairs to get her some jeans, a sweat shirt, socks and her UGG sheepskin boots. When she returned down stairs she noticed Makenzie shaking like a leaf on a tree. She felt helpless knowing there was nothing she could do to stop them from taking her to jail.

The officers allowed Makenzie to change in the small half bathroom right off the kitchen. She closed the door behind her, let down the toilet lid then sat down. She pulled the jeans on, not bothering to remove her pajamas first. She pulled the ripped top over her head and tossed it in the small waste basket next to the sink. Makenzie felt as if all her energy was drained from her body as she pulled both tops over her head.

She played back the incident in her head and scolded herself for not peering through the peephole first, allowing Kalvin to get in the house. He was full of rage and she was terrified that he would kill her this time. As he sat on top of her, she thought about the knife and knew she had to get him before he got her. She'd never forget the look on Kalvin's face when she stabbed him. His evil eyes were replaced with shock and pure fear. The young innocent brother Makenzie once knew appeared across his face and remorse quickly washed over her. She didn't want to kill him. She just wanted him to stop.

A knock at the door interrupted her thoughts. She stood to her feet, hesitantly opened the door and walked out. Officer Scott took her hand cuffs off her belt, positioned Makenzie's hands behind her back then cuffed her.

"You have the right to remain silent. Anything you say…"

"She's just a child. Is that really necessary?" Rhonda asked as Makenzie loudly cried.

"Sorry ma'am, it's procedure," Blair answered.

"Makenzie listen to Mommy. Calm down and do as they say. I'm going to get you out of there. Don't fight the officers. You'll only make it worse. Okay?" Rhonda said, trying to console her daughter.

Makenzie sniffled as she nodded her head up and down.

"I'm going to be driving right behind you, baby."

They walked outside, placed her in the back seat and closed the door.

Gloria Dotson-Lewis

"Where are you taking her?"

"We're taking her to the South Holland station but she'll be transferred to the Juvenile Detention Center on Hamilton in the city. It's late and there's really nothing you can do tonight ma'am.

"What are you saying? She's going to have to stay overnight in that place?"

"I'm afraid so."

chapter 21

The squad car pulled in front of a white building that stood about fourteen stories high. The red sign with white letters identified the building as the Cook County Juvenile Center. Officer Scott got out of the driver's seat, closed her door then opened the rear door behind her. She assisted Makenzie out the car and escorted her to the entrance.

A step-through metal detector greeted them as soon as they walked through the door. It was clear to Makenzie that Officer Scott and Officer Blair were no strangers to this place as they joked around with staff members standing in the lobby.

"What's up Frank? What you doing up here man?" Officer Blair asked the middle aged man with a salt and pepper beard.

"Man, I'm on light duty. You remember that kid Martin you brought in last week? We had to wrestle him down the other day for biting this other kid. That son of a gun kicked me in the ribs."

"Hahaha, what's wrong man? You getting old and can't handle these youngins no more?

"Oh, I can handle myself. You better believe that. That little animal needs to be tied down. He acts like he was raised by a pack of wolves. The ones you bring up in here always seem to be the most trouble. I hope this one here got some sense," he said eyeballing Makenzie as they headed down the hall.

Five minutes after Makenzie arrived, Rhonda rushed through the glass entrance with her hair noticeably out of place. She saw the two officers that were just at her house, leading her daughter down a long hallway.

"That was my daughter that was just brought in. Can you tell me what I need to do to get her out? How much will it cost?" Rhonda asked as she approached the desk.

"She won't be going anywhere tonight. She'll have what's called a detention hearing in the next day or two and at that time the judge will determine if a crime was committed. If no crime was committed then she'll be released but if the judge finds that a crime was committed then a trial date will be set."

"So she may have to spend two nights here? My baby is not a criminal. He attacked her," Rhonda shouted through her tears.

"Just about every parent that comes in here says their child is innocent. We can't just release her because you said so. You'll have to wait until she goes before the judge. If she has to go to trial, the judge may let her go home with an electronic ankle device until her court date, depending on the crime and her criminal history," the gray haired officer explained.

"So, what am I supposed to do now?"

"Go home and get some rest. That's all you can do. Then, call tomorrow to find out the date and time of her hearing," the man replied. "Here is a card with the number on it."

"I can't believe this is happening," she said as she took the card from his hand and walked towards the door. Rhonda didn't know what to do. Her stomach felt like a ball of knots and her knees felt like they were going to buckle from under her. She felt so helpless with all her family living four hours away in Ohio. There was only one person she could call. She took her cell phone out her purse and dialed.

Makenzie was taken to a small room where she was turned over to juvenile police officer Watkins. Officer Watkins stood about 5'7" with a smooth mahogany baby face. Her hair was gelled back into a ponytail that was pinned up into a bun. She had a small waist with a butt that seemed five times too big for her body. Her deep voice was very dry and uncaring and she didn't seem too happy to be there.

After being questioned about the incident, she was taken down the hall to the shower area where she was allowed a quick three minute wash up period. She was given an oversized burgundy pull over shirt that had Property of C.C.J.T.D.C. on the back, tan pants that had the same initials going down the left leg and a pair of footies. She placed her street clothes in a plastic bag along with her boots and handed it to the officer.

Officer Watkins escorted Makenzie down a hall past several classrooms complete with chalkboards and desks, a large gym with a full sized basketball court and a lunch room area that looked similar to the one in her school. Next, they entered a huge open space with chairs, tables and a television in the center. Neatly positioned gym shoes sat outside the doors of each prisoner's room. Makenzie walked past the glass doors, she could see some girls lying across their beds while others stood in the doorway watching her walk by. She was petrified at the thought of having to spend the night there.

Officer Watkins stopped at a door next to a tiny girl who looked no more than eleven years old, sitting on her bed staring at the wall.

"Well, here is your suite for the night," Officer Watkins

said sarcastically as she unlocked the door.

Makenzie's lips curled up at the smell when she entered the small space that held a twin size bed with an ultra thin mattress. The 7x14 inch narrow room had brick walls and no windows. There was a flat pillow positioned on the head of the bed and a cotton blanket at the foot.

"I hope you're not here to stay but if you are, this is what you have the pleasure of waking up to everyday. I don't know what you heard on the streets but this is not a place you wanna be. As you can see it's shut down time around here so I'll see you in the morning."

Officer Watkins stepped out, stuck her key in the lock and bolted it shut. Makenzie watched as she walked towards the security area. She sat on the edge of the bed, covered her face and cried.

What if the judge doesn't believe it was self defense? Will I have to live in this hell hole?

Makenzie got down on her knees and prayed.

God, why does this keep happening to me? I prayed a long time ago not to ever have to see Kalvin again and now this. Please, don't let me go to jail. I was only defending myself. I didn't mean to kill Kalvin. If you get me out of this, I promise never to get in trouble again.

After praying, she sat up until her body was too tired to stay awake. She folded the pillow in half, placed her hand on her right cheek and laid down. She didn't feel comfortable putting her face on a pillowcase someone else could've been drooling on the night before. As she lay there, the attack played over and over in her head until she finally dosed off.

The next morning, Makenzie was escorted in the court room, with handcuffs, by a muscular male officer with freckles. The small court room was filled with parents waiting to hear their child's fate. Faces of despair and worry covered the space like a dark cloud hovering over the sky. It was so quiet you could hear folks breathing.

Makenzie was dressed in the street clothes she wore to the station the night of the attack. Her hair was brushed in a ponytail that sat high on the back of her head and her face was void of any makeup. She looked around the room for a familiar face, spotted her mom in the third row and started crying.

"I wanna go home ma. I don't wanna . . ."

Bam . . . Bam . . . Bam . . .

"Order in the court, order in the court."

Makenzie turned from her mother to face the judge behind the elevated oak wood desk. Her stomach immediately dropped when she saw the same judge who just six months before told her he better not see her back in his court room.

This situation really wasn't her fault and she hoped he wouldn't punish her now for what she did to Jordan. She stood there in silence, glancing back a couple of times to look at her mother.

"Ms. Pierce, I see you're back in my court room again. You just can't stay on the right side of the law," the judge said as he looked up from the paperwork in front of him.

"But, it really wasn't my fault this time. My brother..."

"The last time you were here you said it wasn't your fault. Your problem is, you don't like to own up to your bad choices and I'm sure that's why you're here in front of me again. I consider myself to be a fair judge and I believe in second chances but I don't like it when people don't take me seriously," he said with one eyebrow raised.

"What was I supposed to do? Let him kill me? Then would you believe me?" Makenzie screamed through tears.

Bam . . . Bam . . . Bam . . .

Gloria Dotson-Lewis

"I want you to be quiet and listen. I see girls like you in my court room every day. You're disrespectful and you have a hardhead. You think it's cute to talk back and fight and the only way girls like you learn is the hard way. You won't get it together until I take away your freedom."

"Please, believe me. I swear, he attacked me," Makenzie cried. She felt like she was being jabbed in the stomach.

"Was there someone else there with you that can confirm what you're saying?" He said as he lowered his head to glance over his glasses.

"Yes . . . I mean no," Makenzie thought about her father but knew he wouldn't tell the court the truth. He jumped in the ambulance with Kalvin and didn't even look back once to see about her.

"Which one is it Ms. Pierce? Yes or no?"

"No, I guess," Makenzie said after taking a deep breath. She dropped her eyes to the floor in defeat.

"Well, what you did this time is much more serious than the others. You can't pay a fine and walk away from this. You stabbed someone," the judge lectured.

"Your Honor I was there. I saw the whole thing," a voice shouted from the back of the room.

Makenzie turned around to see her father standing in the last row near the door. She couldn't believe this was happening to her. Her father had stood by when she was twelve and let her brother get away with raping her and now he was there to have her put away. She wondered if his showing up was revenge for her killing Kalvin.

"And, who are you?" Judge Kowalczyk questioned.

"I'm Walter Pierce, Makenzie's father. I'm also the father of the victim."

Several bystanders gasped for air and began whispering at the news. Rhonda turned to see her ex-husband standing in the aisle. He had on the same blue jeans and black polo shirt he had on yesterday. His eyes were blood shot red and his short wavy hair looked like it hadn't been combed in days.

"Can I approach sir," Walter asked.

"Ok, come up then. Tell me what happened."

Walter looked at Makenzie then back at the judge. "I heard my daughter yelling when I walked up to the door. I tried the door and it was unlocked so I rushed in. I saw my son Kalvin on top of my daughter as she struggled to get loose. He punched her and before I could get to them Makenzie reached for a knife on the floor near them and stabbed him once," he lied.

"So you're saying that you witnessed your son attempting to assault your daughter then she stabbed him in self-defense?" The judge asked.

"That's what I'm saying Your Honor."

Makenzie couldn't believe her father was coming to her rescue. She saw a tear race down his face when he looked over at her. Makenzie looked away not sure how to feel about her father.

"I know that Makenzie has done some not so smart things in the eye of the law but this Your Honor is all on my son. I didn't get a chance to tell the police officers that because I thought my son was dying so I went to the hospital with him. He had to have a blood transfusion but other than that he'll be fine. I'm just saying he should be here not Makenzie," Walter insisted.

"Well then, if that's the case, self-dense is not a crime so Makenzie Pierce you'll be released in the custody of your parents today. But, you are to continue your counseling sessions as ordered in the previous case and in doing so I hope you get the help you need for this situation as well," the judge said to Makenzie.

Makenzie closed her eyes, thanked God and started crying in relief. She turned to look at her mother who had her hands weaved together touching her lips in a praying position.

"Mr. Pierce, we're going to send an officer over to the hospital to stand guard until your son is released. He'll be taken into custody for assault."

"Yes, Your Honor. I understand," Mr. Walter said. "Can I ask you a question, sir?"

"Go ahead."

"I umm, I'm ashamed to say that I was involved in a crime four years ago. I know that if I had done the right thing back then, we wouldn't be here today. My daughter has been suffering all these years because of me. I didn't protect her like I should have. When she was only twelve, I walked in on my son, Kalvin raping Makenzie and I didn't have him arrested. I took the law into my own hands. I was a horrible father and I want to turn myself in today for covering up that crime?" Walter stood there trembling.

The courtroom erupted.

Bam . . . Bam . . . Bam . . .

"Order, order in the court," the judge yelled.

"You definitely need to turn yourself in but not here. This is a juvenile court system. You can report to the nearest police station and they'll take your statement and go from there."

"Thank you," Walter said as he turned to walk away. He glanced at Makenzie and mouthed the words, "I'm sorry" before heading through the double doors.

Everything happened so quickly. One minute Makenzie pictured herself spending time in jail for killing her brother and the next minute, she was being released. She was in a state of shock over the actions of her father. He came through for her and she knew that without his statement, it would've been her word against Kalvin's. She just couldn't figure out why. All she knew was at that moment she was thankful because Judge Kowalczyk was ready to send her back to juvie.

"Ms. Pierce."

Makenzie snapped from her thoughts and turned her attention back to the judge. "Yes, Your Honor?"

"I'm glad to see you get to go home. I just hope I don't see you back here. You're getting a second chance that a lot of kids that come through here don't get. I hope you stay out of trouble."

"You won't see me back here," Makenzie said as she looked around the room. "I don't ever wanna see this place again."

chapter aa

"Don't you look lovely," Dr. Reid said to Makenzie as she sat across from her in her usual spot on the couch.

Makenzie looked down at her outfit as if she forgot what she had on. The black pencil skirt stopped right above her knees. Her white button down blouse was tucked in at the waist and slightly opened at the neck. An oversized black belt hugged her midsection, while silver studded earrings and a matching necklace added to her professional attire.

"Thank you. I actually just came from a job interview at Forever 21 in Orland Mall," Makenzie smiled.

"That's great. How do you think it went?"

"Let's just say I think I'll be getting a second interview," Makenzie laughed.

"Confident aren't we," Dr. Reid smiled. "So, what else is going on?"

"Oh, Dr. Reid, so much has happened in the last couple of months. I really do miss our sessions. Let's see, where do I start? Well, I told you about my father showing up the day Kalvin attacked me. I couldn't figure out at the time what he was doing there. But, come to find out, after the group session with my mother, she went by my grandmother's house looking for my father but he wasn't there. I don't know what she was strapped with but from what Malkomb said, she wasn't there to just talk. She was mad and ready to hurt somebody. She told Grandma P what her son and grandson did to me and threatened to kill them both. Anyway, my dad turned himself in the day after he told the judge that I was innocent. They gave him a year but mom says he may only do half of that."

"I'm so glad your father and brother wasn't home at the time. Sometimes we get caught up in our emotions and do things we can't take back. How do you feel about your father's sentence?"

"I used to say he should be locked up for the rest of his life for what he did to me. He was my dad. He was supposed to protect me but he didn't. I mean, this may sound strange but I was always more hurt by what my dad did than by what Kalvin did to me. When he turned his back on me my world was flipped upside down. I have not been the same since. But, now that he's locked up, I feel sorry for him. Isn't that weird?" Makenzie said as she swept a tear from her face. "Don't get me wrong I'm still mad at him."

"It's not weird. It's normal to feel mixed emotions when someone you love has hurt you. And, it's natural for you to feel sad that he's in a bad situation."

"I guess," Makenzie mumbled as she hunched her shoulders. "He wrote me from jail but it took me a week to open it. I didn't want to hear anything he had to say, not even through a letter. But after walking past the envelope so many times my curiosity got the best of me. I didn't know if he was writing to apologize or maybe he felt like he'd made the wrong decision telling the judge that it was self defense."

Dr. Reid sat up straight giving Makenzie her full attention. She nodded to let her know she had her full attention.

"My hands were shaking so much while I was opening it," Makenzie smirked and shook her head. "I opened it and there were only two sentences on the paper. Will you please come visit me? I want to talk to you face to face."

"Do you plan on going?" Dr. Reid asked before crossing her arms.

"I don't know if I want to. Why should I talk to him now after all these years? When I needed him, he wasn't there and now he's locked up and lonely and has all the time in the world for me. Really? I don't think so," Makenzie snapped as she rolled her eyes.

"Well, that's definitely a decision you have to make. But, maybe it could help you get some closure on things that have been lingering in your mind and on your heart all this time. He wants to talk to you but maybe you can write down some questions for him to answer."

Makenzie shook her head as she bit her nail. "I never thought about that. I'll have to think about it some more."

"What's going on with your brother's case?"

"He's in jail with my dad waiting for the trial to begin. He pleaded not guilty at his hearing. His bail was set at $100,000 but no one paid his bail so he'll have to stay in there until his trial date. Unfortunately, I'll have to go back and forth to court dealing with that whole thing which makes me sick on the stomach just thinking about it. But, I'm going to do whatever it takes because that bastard needs to be under the jail. Oops, I'm sorry Dr. Reid," Makenzie said as she covered her mouth.

"It's okay sweetie. I know how upset you get talking about him. How are you and your mom doing?"

"We're good, much better than we were. She doesn't get on my nerves as much as she used to. We've been hanging out together a little more and I actually enjoy it. I guess I got over blaming her for not knowing what happened."

Dr. Reid smiled at the noticeably changed young lady in front of her.

You Got Me Twisted

"I also finally went to see my Grandma P. I hadn't seen her since my father was locked up. She's really close to my dad and Kalvin so I was afraid of what she had to say. But, she cried and apologized over and over like all of it was her fault. Malkomb said they had to take her to the hospital for chest pains when she first found out but everything came back fine. She's still really pissed at them and refuses to visit either of them in jail. I go visit her at least once a week now to make sure she's okay.

"Well, that's fantastic Makenzie. I'm so happy for you. It sounds like you've made a lot of progress," Dr. Reid smiled.

"I write a lot more now. It helps me to get my true feelings out in the open. I was convincing myself that I was fine and everyone else had the problem but now I know some things are on me."

"I'm so proud of you young lady."

"I also set some goals like you told me and posted them on my wall so I can look at them every day. One of them is to apologize to a few people I know I hurt. I just have to figure out the right words to say."

"Good for you." Dr. Reid smiled. "I remember when you first started coming to see me, you where such a tough girl. You would roll your eyes and make sarcastic comments or sometimes you'd just refuse to talk at all but now look at you."

"Yeah, I didn't like you at first. I thought you just were some random lady who wanted to be all up in my business," Makenzie laughed. "But, thanks to you, I'm free.

"You did all the work. I just helped pull it out of you. You're brave and strong and you have such a bright future ahead of you.

"If it weren't for you, I probably would've taken that secret to my grave. No one understands me the way you do.

Gloria Dotson-Lewis

Thanks for everything. I'll never forget you."

Makenzie stood to her feet, walked the few steps that separated them and wrapped her arms around Dr. Reid.

chapter 23

Makenzie and Mya were starving so they headed over to Italian Fiesta Pizzeria down the street from their school. They had just started offering pizza by the slice a couple of months prior so it was usually packed with other students. They crossed the street in the center of Cottage Grove Avenue, walked to 154th Street then stopped and waited for oncoming traffic to pass.

Patrons busied the shopping center that also housed a Fairway Finer Foods, Harold's Chicken Shack and Video Village. As they walked across the parking lot, Mya pulled Makenzie out of harm's way as a silver Jeep Cherokee headed their way.

The small restaurant had no seating space and only offered food to go. A huge bulletproof glass plate divided the employees from the customers. Makenzie glanced around the crowded room and spotted Issayah and Chris standing against the far wall. She saw Issayah just about every day in school but avoided him whenever possible. They hadn't spoken since the altercation between her and Robyn in the hallway.

She really liked Issayah and hated how things ended. She still thought about him all the time. Counseling helped her to realize that she mistreated him. She wanted to call him on many occasions to apologize but couldn't get up the nerve.

"Girl, Issayah and Chris are here," Makenzie whispered to Mya.

Mya leaned forward and looked their way. Chris was

looking at her so she waved. He walked over and hugged them both.

"What's up M and M?"

"You are such a lame," Mya laughed.

"What ya'll up too?" Chris asked.

"Umm, what does it look like? We're getting something to eat," Mya responded.

"Girl, you know you got a smart mouth. You're the only one I let get away with it."

"Why is Issayah acting all funny? My girl ain't tripping on him anymore. He don't have to stand all the way over there," Mya said as she twisted her neck.

"Ya'll need to ask him that."

Makenzie moved up to the window, ordered a slice of cheese pizza and paid for her food. She stepped over and retrieved her pizza from the revolving window. After stealing a peak of Issayah she took a position near the door and waited for Mya.

Issayah walked in Makenzie's direction. This was her opportunity to apologize. She cleared her throat.

"I'll wait outside man," Issayah said to Chris before walking out.

Makenzie couldn't take it anymore. She needed to talk to him today. She departed the restaurant then looked around until she spotted Issayah leaning against his car navigating through his cell phone. She strolled over and stopped just inches away.

"Hi Issayah," she said as she bit her thumb nail.

"Sup," he quickly looked up then back down as he answered.

"Can I talk to you?"

"About what?"

"I umm, want to apologize to you." Makenzie cleared her

throat then took a deep breath.

Issayah folded his arms across his chest and tilted his head to the side as he made eye contract.

"I did some things that were stupid."

"What kinds of things?" Issayah taunted.

It was hard for Makenzie to finally get up the nerve to approach Issayah to apologize and all he was doing was making it harder for her. Between the nonchalant facial expressions and sarcastic remarks, she started to believe maybe it wasn't a good idea. But, then again, she had done some terrible things to him and deserved what he was dishing out.

"I umm, I'm sorry for embarrassing you at Beggars, for disrespecting you and for putting my hands on you. Hitting you was out of order and it should never had happened. I didn't know how to handle my anger so I took it out on you and you didn't deserve that. What I did at Beggars was so low and I understand why you dumped me. I think about things when it's too late and I realize that now," Makenzie nervously spoke as she rubbed her sweaty palms together.

"Man, I should've recorded this."

"Okay, whatever Issayah. I said what I had to say but I see it's a big joke to you." Makenzie turned to walk back towards the pizzeria. Issayah gently grabbed her arm.

"It's cool shorty. I was just messing with you. I know how stubborn you are so it must have been hard for you to step to me. We're cool."

Makenzie lightly slapped him on the arm. "Boy, why you playing me like that?

"Didn't wanna let you get off too easy," Issayah laughed. "Give me a hug."

Makenzie hugged him around the neck. She closed her eyes and took a deep breath. It felt so good to be in his arms like old times. She really did miss him.

"So we're cool, right? Does that mean you won't ignore me in school anymore?" Makenzie asked as she stepped out of his embrace.

"I guess," Issayah joked. "Naw, we're good.

"Woohoo!" Mya shouted as she witnessed them hugging. They both looked in her direction and shook their heads. Mya and Chris walked over to the car. Thirty minutes flew by as they stood around talking and laughing.

"Your girl finally agreed to let me take her out," Chris said.

"What? I can't believe it."

"Yeah, I hope don't no crazy chick pop up out of a bush trying to tear my head off."

"Girl, you tripping, I ain't thinking about none of these biscuit head girls up here. I've been trying to get with you since last year."

"Maybe we can make it a double date," Issayah said looking at Makenzie.

"That would be cool." Makenzie looked at him with a subtle smile. She tried to remain calm as the Fourth of July fireworks went off inside her body.

Makenzie saw three girls heading their way and immediately recognized Robyn. She was with her girls so she knew Robyn would be trying to act tough even though Makenzie had already kicked her butt once.

Robyn was wearing her school jogging pants with the matching hoodie with some all white gym shoes. She walked up, looked Makenzie and Mya up and down then spoke to Issayah and Chris. Makenzie and Mya looked at each other and shook their heads.

"What's up fellas?"

"What's up?" Issayah and Chris said in unison.

You Got Me Twisted

"What ya'll on later tonight? We're going up to Beggars. Ya'll wanna meet up there?" Robyn asked.

"Yeh, we'll be up there around 8p.m.," Paris chimed in.

"I'll hit you up if we head that way," Issayah answered.

"Okay, I hope you do," Robyn flirted.

Robyn turned towards Makenzie. "I would invite you two but you're probably barred from coming back up there after that last incident," Robyn and her girls laughed.

"You have a really big mouth for someone who can't back it up," Makenzie said.

"That wasn't a fair fight. I wasn't expecting you to get ghetto over a few words. You caught me off guard."

"If that's what helps you get over the butt whooping I gave you then you keep going with that."

"Man, ya'll need to chill," Issayah jumped in.

"Get your girl then," Mya said.

"Ain't nobody even talking to you," Paris moved closer.

"It's cool Mya. Let's go. I'm not in the mood to give her a beat down today," Makenzie said.

Makenzie was surprisingly calm. Any other time she would've laid Robyn's big mouth butt out by now. She was ecstatic that Issayah had accepted her apology and she wasn't about to let Robyn mess that up.

"Issayah, I'll talk to you later; you too Chris," Makenzie said before turning to walk away. Mya said her goodbyes then caught up with her girl.

"I can't believe you didn't steal on her. She talks too darn much. I started to beat her down myself."

"She's not worth it. The po-pos be riding through here all the time. I'm just not trying to get in anymore trouble. Besides, Issayah and I are just friends and we're cool again. That's all I care about. She's not even a factor."

"Wow, that Dr. Reid lady you always talking about must

really be helping you.

"I guess you can say that," Makenzie smiled.

chapter 24

"Y ou know, I think you're really strong and brave," Rhonda said to Makenzie as they headed north on the Dan Ryan Expressway.

"I don't feel strong."

"Well, you are. You have been through so much but you never let it break you down. I hate you had to go through all of that alone but I'm glad that you finally got it out. It's brought us closer and I'm enjoying the time that we are now spending together. I feel like we missed out on a lot," she said, as she quickly glanced over at her daughter then back to the road.

"That was my fault. I not only blamed Kalvin and dad, I blamed you too. I guess I thought you should've had some psychic ability to read into my mind and figure things out," Makenzie said as she shook her head.

"Don't blame yourself. None of this was your fault. "

"I said and did a lot of things to you and I'm sorry. You didn't deserve that."

"You don't owe me anything sweetheart.

"Yes, I do. I remember saying a lot of disrespectful things to you. I at least owe you those two small words."

"Okay then, I accept your apology. You seem like a different person now; happier. That's all that matters now," Rhonda said as she took her right hand off the steering wheel and placed it on Makenzie left thigh.

"Thanks, I wish I could take back some of those things I said."

Gloria Dotson-Lewis

Rhonda's heart filled with joy as she listened to her daughter. She couldn't believe the drastic change she'd made. They laughed and talked all the time now. They went to the movies and even went shopping together. They truly enjoyed each other's company and Rhonda felt like she had her real daughter back.

They pulled into the parking lot across the street from the Cook County Correctional Facility on 26th and California. They gathered their belongings then crossed the busy intersection. Once inside they were immediately searched then handed their photo identifications cards to the guard.

After waiting several minutes, they were given directions and rules to follow while there then asked to stand in a straight-line formation. They followed a big bellied male officer down the hall to a long, narrow room. The room had beige walls with plenty of lighting. Small cubicles stretched from one end of the room to the other. Round wooden stools with matching desk tops rested in front of thick glass windows. A black telephone receiver hung on the right side at each area.

"I'm so nervous," Makenzie said as she sat on her assigned stool with her mother standing over her.

"If you want to leave now we can. No one is forcing you to do this. You just say the word. You don't owe him anything. You never have to see him again if you don't want to."

"No, I want to . . . I need to. I have some unanswered questions for him."

"Okay but if at any time you feel uncomfortable you let me know and we can get out of here."

"I know mom."

Makenzie knew her mother didn't really want her to come. She was extremely upset over this whole situation and blamed the whole thing on her father. Her father had called collect a few times from jail and Makenzie heard her mother cursing him out with words she had never heard her mother even use before.

Makenzie's eyes were redirected to the opening door on the opposite side of the glass. A group of prisoners strolled through the entrance in their one piece orange jumpsuits. They looked through every window in search of their loved ones.

Makenzie was in awe of a man who had to bend down to get through the door. He stood at least seven feet tall with muscular arms covered in tattoos. His jumpsuit dangled above his ankles and his bald head shined like the sun. When he looked through her window, Makenzie quickly turned away. He looked like someone straight out a horror movie.

When she looked back up, she saw her father coming through the door. She bit the corner of her lip as she nervously twirled the watch on her wrist. As Makenzie observed him, she immediately noticed that he had lost some weight but his beer belly was still expanding the front of his jumpsuit. His normally trimmed beard was untamed and his almond shaped eyes where a dull off white color.

Walter spotted Makenzie and locked eyes with her for a few seconds. He dropped his head as he walked over to the window and sat on the stool in front of her. He picked up the phone on his side of the cubicle and pointed for her to pick up the one on her side. Makenzie slowly removed it from the hook and placed it on her ear.

"Hi sweetheart, thanks for coming. You look beautiful," Walter said as he looked through the glass at his daughter.

"I didn't come for you, I did it for me."

"Ok, well I'm glad you decided to come. I umm . . .

wanted to talk to you and I didn't think it could wait until I get out."

"Ok . . . I'm here. What's up?"

"I know it's way overdue but I want to apologize. I made a bad decision."

"A bad decision? Is that what you call what you did?"

"I'm sorry Makenzie. I messed up. I didn't know what to do."

"You knew exactly what you should've done but you chose not to. You chose to protect him and abandon me," Makenzie shouted in the receiver.

Rhonda rubbed Makenzie on the shoulder to calm her. A guard walked in their direction to see what the commotion was then walked back after he saw things were under control.

"It wasn't like that. I thought of the military as a form of punishment for him but I also thought they could straighten him out. I didn't want him to end up in jail with all those grown men that would probably hurt him or worse, kill him."

"You mean hurt him like he hurt me? He deserved whatever he would've got in jail."

"You're right. I wish I had it to do all over again but I don't. I know you're upset and you have every right to be. But, I hope one day you'll find it in your heart to forgive me," he said, as he looked her in her eyes.

"It's been almost four years and now you want me to forgive you? Now that you're locked up and feeling sorry for yourself, I'm supposed to forgive you? What you're suffering now couldn't be half of what I've been going through all these years," Makenzie brushed her tears away like a windshield wiper on high speed.

"You're right. I could be in here the rest of my life and it still wouldn't compare to the pain we've caused you. I could never in a million years make up for what I did. I can only apologize and pray that you'll forgive me."

"I loved you and you left me when I needed you the most. You told me not to tell anyone and I didn't but you still left me. Did you blame me or something?"

"No, not at all. I loved you so much and I still do. I stayed away because I was ashamed of what I did, not because I didn't love you. I didn't protect you and that made me feel worthless. Every time I looked at you I felt guilty. I started drinking because I didn't know how to handle the pain and guilt."

Makenzie saw her father's eyes fill with tears. She tried to fight the sympathy she felt in her heart for him with anger. She didn't want him to get off that easy. He didn't deserve her sympathy. He needed to suffer the consequences for the choices he made. She thought about that day and got angry all over again. Rhonda stood silently as her daughter got everything off her chest.

"You should feel guilty," Makenzie coldly said into the phone. "You should have done the right thing. Tell me something, did you remain close to Kalvin over the years?"

"No. I was angry at him for doing what he did to you. I couldn't get the image out my head. I couldn't stand my own son and I couldn't talk to anyone about it. I blamed myself to and felt that maybe I did something wrong as a father. He would write me from different countries while he was in the military but I never wrote back. I couldn't pretend that nothing happened," he said as he shook his head side to side.

When Kalvin attacked her this last time, he blamed her for their dad hating him and now she knew what he meant. All this time, Makenzie thought her father had chosen

Kalvin over her. But now she knew that wasn't the case and it made her feel a little better. She was glad to hear that she wasn't the only one suffering over the past four years but deep down inside she was happier to know her father never stopped loving her. Makenzie was overcome with emotion and couldn't take anymore.

"Look, I'm about to be out. Are you finished?" Makenzie stood to her feet with the phone still in her hand.

"I love you, Makenzie and I always will. I want you to know that just in case you decide never to talk to me again. What I did was unforgivable and I understand why you hate me. I didn't want to go another day without telling you how I really feel. And, I'm going to pray every day that one day you'll forgive me."

Makenzie hung up the phone as she looked deeply into her father's eyes. She saw what she knew was sincerity and it warmed her cold heart. She knew right then she would forgive him but she just didn't know when.

Discussion Questions

1. Do you think it's ever okay for a person to physically put his/her hands on their partner out of anger? If yes, when?

2. Do you agree with Makenzie that Jordan was part to blame for what she did to his car?

3. Why do you think Makenzie became so angry that she resorted to physical violence time after time?

4. Makenzie was mad at her mother for years because she felt she should've known that she was sexually abused. Do you agree?

5. Robyn deliberately did things to make Makenzie jealous. Do you think Robyn got what she deserved in the school hallway?

6. Was Robyn right when she called Makenzie insecure or did Makenzie have a right to go off on Robyn for calling Issayah on the weekend?

7. When Mr. Pierce walked in on Kalvin raping Makenzie, do you think he should've called the police right then and there or do you see his view on why he felt the need to send him to the military instead?

8. Do you think Makenzie should forgive her father? Why or why not?

9. Do you think a young man who is being abused by his girlfriend is weak or is it just as serious as when a young lady is being abused by her boyfriend?

10. Do you think you would know if one of your friends was being abused by his/her partner and hiding it? If yes, what are some of the signs?

11. If you discover your friend or loved one is being abused what would you say to him or her if anything?

12. If you are being abused by your partner do you know who to contact to get help?

About the Author

Gloria Dotson-Lewis is a married mother of three. She was born and raised on the Southside of Chicago and is currently pursuing a degree in Social

Work. Her future endeavor is to start a not-for-profit organization for teen girls to empower them with self-esteem, confidence, and strong decision-making skills in hopes of giving them the tools they need to enhance their future as leaders of tomorrow.

Gloria enjoys writing true to life fiction stories for teens that not only entertain but also evoke positive messages.

Visit her online at www.gloriadotsonlewis.com or email her at gdotsonlewis@gmail.com

Domestic Abuse Assistance

If you need help or you just want more information about domestic abuse call the number below or visit one of the websites listed.

National Domestic Violence Hotline: 1-800-799-SAFE (7233)

www.thehotline.org
or
www.loveisrespect.org

Sexual Assault Assistance

If you need help or you just want more information about sexual abuse call the number below or visit the website listed.

National Sexual Assault Hotline: 1-800-656-HOPE (4673)

http://www.rainn.org/get-help/national-sexual-assault-hotline

** IF YOU ARE BEING ABUSED IN ANYWAY, TELL SOMEONE YOU TRUST.**

WAHIDA CLARK PRESENTS
YOUNG ADULT
BEST SELLING TITLES

Under Pressure by Rashawn Hughes

The Boy Is Mines! By Charmaine White

Ninety-nine Problems Gloria Dotson-Lewis

Sade's Secret by Sparkle

Player Hater by Charmaine White

ON SALE NOW!

www.wcpyoungadult.com

60 Evergreen Place Suite 904 East Orange NJ 07018

973.678.9982

WAHIDA CLARK PRESENTS

A Young Adult Novel BY

GLORIA DOTSON-LEWIS

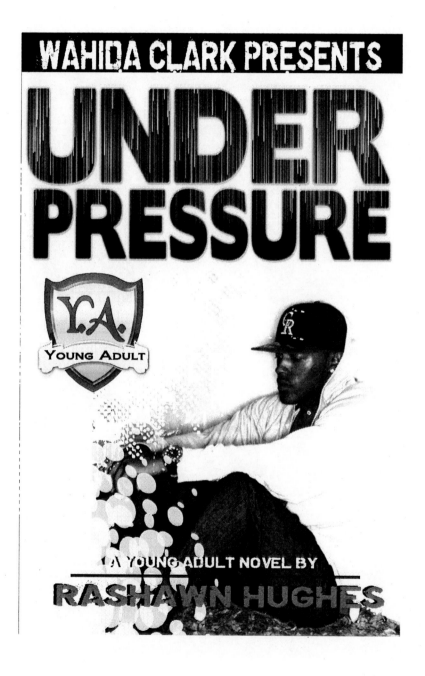

WAHIDA CLARK PRESENTS

UNDER PRESSURE

YOUNG ADULT

A YOUNG ADULT NOVEL BY

RASHAWN HUGHES

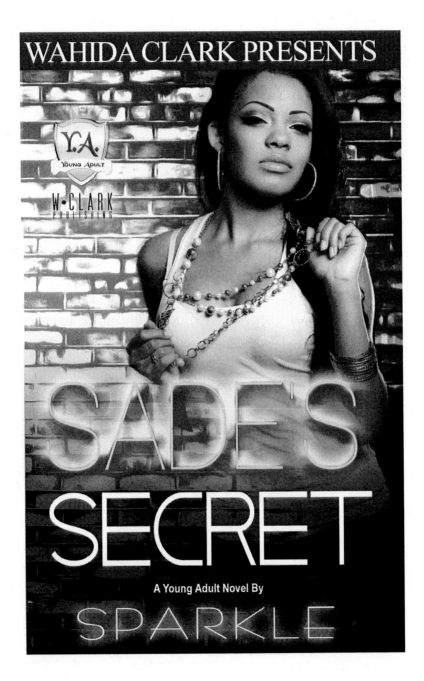

WAHIDA CLARK PRESENTS

Y.A.
YOUNG ADULT

W·CLARK
PUBLISHING

SADE'S
SECRET

A Young Adult Novel By

SPARKLE

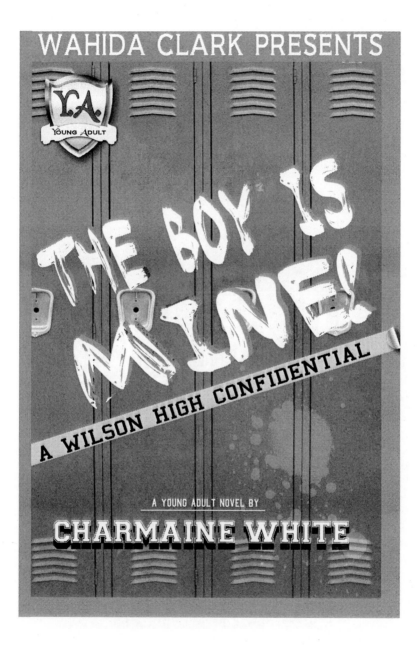

WAHIDA CLARK PRESENTS

YOUNG ADULT

THE BOY IS MINE!

A WILSON HIGH CONFIDENTIAL

A YOUNG ADULT NOVEL BY

CHARMAINE WHITE

WAHIDA CLARK PRESENTS

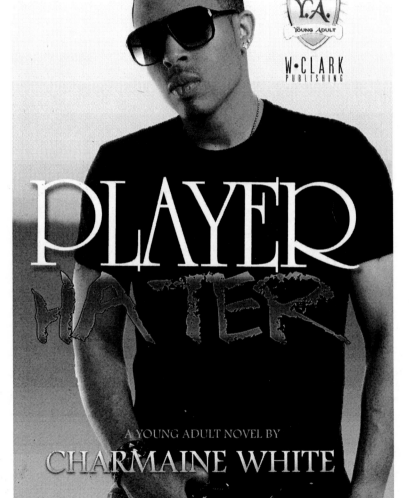

A YOUNG ADULT NOVEL BY

CHARMAINE WHITE